Paul Katsitis

Mikonos Crime 1
Abducted

Paul Katsitis

Mikonos Crime one

Abducted

So far in this series appeared:

Mykonos Crime 1 Abducted
Mykonos Crime 2 Confusion (Feb 20)
Mykonos Crime 3 The Prince (Feb 20)

Published in German and Greek:
Mykonos Crime 1 Die Bestie von Mykonos
Mykonos Crime 2 Rache
Mykonos Crime 4 Der Drei-Sterne-Mord
Mykonos Crime 5 Tattoo
Mykonos Crime 6 Skalpell
Mykonos Crime 7 Hass
Mykonos Crime 8 Sturm über Mykonos
Mykonos Crime 9 Die Maske
Mykonos Crime 10 Abseits
Mykonos Crime 11 Glut
Mykonos Crime 12 Putsch
Mykonos Crime 13 Royals
Mykonos Crime 14 Traumata
Mykonos Crime 15 Khaled
Mykonos Crime 16 Sisa

English and German/Greek volumes have different numbers!

imprint
Cover picture: Gest. Katsitis / Porträtaufn.
deep kircher
Copyright Paul Katsitis 2019
Herstellung und Verlag: BoD- Books on Demand
Norderstedt

ISBN 9783750418998

Unfortunately, many gay books remain unpublished because translation costs are high and publishing is therefore unprofitable. So I asked a Greek friend who was born in London to translate the series. He is not a professional translator.
So come across mistakes: smile and read on. And remember: His English is certainly better than your Greek :)
Thanks, Antonis!

Each volume deals with a completed case, so the volumes do not need to be read in order.

All the books of the series were set in Greece. Since Greek typesetters cannot detect any mistakes in English, there are certainly more mistakes in the book than in a normal book. But so at least a few euros remain in Greece.

Alexandros Nikakis (formerly Galis), 36, is senior commissioner in Mikonos and is married to

Angelos Nikakis, 30, who was the chief commissioner in Thessaloniki.
They felt in love and decided to open a private detective agency on Mikonos. In order to save the costs of a commissioner and deputy, Alex and Angelos determine on behalf of the community in murder cases. A good deal for both sides.
For a year, now, Angelos is also mayor.
I forgot - they married 7 days after they met.

1
Istanbul

Safiye scurried through the door and closed it quickly.
"Sister," Khaled called joyfully. The siblings kissed and rejoiced over the meeting.
"How did you escape the vultures?" Khaled asked.
"You know, there are times when Arab women have to be alone. Neither a sheikh nor bodyguards should be allowed to override the laws of the Koran", Safiye smiled.
"And that would be?" Khaled asked with a smile.
"The sauna followed by a massage. I just have to wet my hair! "
She had to learn quickly that such trifles mattered if she wanted to maintain her already limited range of motion.
Khaled put his arm around her and led her to the couch.
"Your burdocks are not there?", asked Safiye.
"It's not that bad for me. They just have to protect me from terrorists, not from men in general. I sent them to the embassy to pick up important documents that need guarding. The documents always come from myself. I always send them before departure! "

Safiye burst out laughing.

"Good trick. I have to remember", she said.

"Now tell me how you are. We have not seen each other in months", Khaled said.

"Because you're on the road all the time", Safiye replied.

"You know exactly why. At home I am under constant guard. I cannot take one step alone. I still curse my brother today. Even though I somehow regret his death. It got me into this office. I never wanted and I do not want to!"

"You're in a better position than me. It's like having chains on my foot. But do not worry. Our father will rule out of the coffin!"

Khaled laughed.

"You're right. Without him the world goes under - he thinks. And he will not die under warranty before you are married. I'm surprised he has not presented you a husband! "

"He already has", Safiye said sadly.

"WHAT?"

'Two weeks ago. What do you think, why I fled!"

"Who is it?"

'The son of the sheikh of Ajman!"

"He's over forty! And besides, a second-degree relative! That's when the kids will ... "

"Stupid you mean? Well, neither of us are stupid, even though Mother's father is a cousin! "

"You're right. I'm just looking for an argument
to prevent this nonsense", said Khaled angrily.
"How do you want to prevent it? Does he at
least look good?"
"He looks like his father!"
"As fat and with a hooked nose", Khaled
stated.
"He is just ugly. The thought of sex ... ",
she could not speak further because she
burst into tears. Khaled sat down next to her
and put his arm around her.
"I promise, I will think of something.
A word of honor by your brother!"
Safiye smiled a little.
"Everyone always thinks we lead a carefree
life. Luxury yes. Freedom no!", Khaled wailed.
"Wait. It will not be long, then Father wants
that I get married. Thankfully, Father believes
that I must first visit as many countries as
possible. I'm very grateful for that! "
Khaled burst out laughing.
"What you really do in these countries ..."
"If he ever finds out, he'll kill me", Khaled said.
"Great. I cannot think of something like that.
Imagine, I'm no longer a virgin at the
wedding! "
Khaled laughed again.
"I would like to see Father's face!"
"Not me", Safiye replied, but also had to grin.
"Nice that you're here", Khaled said honestly.
"And at least partially in freedom!"

"But I'm not the only one who has problems. What about you?"

"Oh, Safiye. I try not to think about it. I do not know how it will end well for me", Khaled complained.

"There we are already two. After all, I'm allowed to go one week to Mikonos! "

"In this den of inquinity? Does father know about it?"

"Naturally. He does not want to know anything about women's issues, especially when dealing with the body. And I told him I could not get it at home because the media could get wind of it. So he agreed to the trip. Of course, under the strictest watch. But I'm already out of it! "

Khaled grinned. That would be her destiny.

"The goal is a clinic on Mikonos?"

"Exactly!"

"I hope you can have some fun, little sister!"

"Under warranty. And you have a lot of fun in Istanbul. For what reason are you here? ", asked Safiye.

"A Conference on Artificial Intelligence. I will not understand a word! "

"Artificial intelligence. Well, our family needs a lot ", Safiye said with a laugh.

"No. Even that does not help! "

Both laughed.

"Khaled, I have to go back to the room. My burdocks will be restless otherwise!"

"Now? Too bad. Do not forget to moisten the hair! "
"I almost forgot that now," Safiye said, kissing Khaled.

Khaled, 26, was the Crown Prince of the Emirate of Sharjah.
And Safiye his two years older sister.

2
Mikonos, 13 nautical miles east

Victor Poroshenko looked at his monitor on the bridge of "Subsea 7".
"We'll get to the target," said the captain to his first officer.
"Yes, another twenty seconds!"
The captain nodded.
It was a roaring hot day and calm.
Poroshenko also knew the Aegean Sea differently. When the north wind, coming from Poroshenko's homeland, Ukraine, swings

southwards, it becomes a wind monster.
Mistral or Bora are a breeze against it.
More than once he had come into heavy
seas and with much larger ships than the
almost delicate "Subsea 7".
"Anchor!" He called and picked up the
phone.
"Final position reached. You can start, Brown!
"
Shortly thereafter, the Filipinos scurried across
the deck.
Poroshenko liked his Filipinos. No wonder they
are felt to be found on every ship in the world
- they are reliable, hard-working and fast, he
thought. Maybe because they are so small.
He smiled.
After only ten minutes, they had painted over
the ship's name, the color being almost
directly dried on the brush because it was so
hot.
Then you attached the sheet metal sign.
Poroshenko had to laugh out loud.
The gentlemen in Houston had humor. The
"Subsea 7" became the "Ocean Saver". The
only thing missing was that we hoist the
"Greenpeace" flag, he thought.
It was very smart to send the Subsea 7 to the
Aegean, because it looked different from
any other exploration ship. They usually had a
winding tower as a structure. A floating
drilling tower, which was immediately
recognizable as such. The "Subsea 7",

however, did not have this structure. From the many protests they had learned that you have to make such ships visually different in order to drill in peace.

And so the "Subsea 7" looked more like a marine-biological ship or a high-tech fishtrawler. Since then, the cinnabar was over. Chains of fishing boats, rubber dinghies from Greenpeace and WWF, and how those idiots are all called, brawls between the Filipinos and local fishermen - all history. It went unnoticed and the name change, albeit illegal, added a small portion to the reassurance. An "ocean saver" must have something to do with environmental protection. Simply because humans expect it because of the name. If the name "oil spinner" would be denounced on the ship, one would not need to enter a port.

Shortly thereafter, the little ship vibrated, but Poroshenko had been used to it for years.

The first test hole. Not even an hour after reaching the position. Time is money. Each operating hour of "Subsea 7" costs $ 16,000. And there were many other jobs that needed to be done. Since the natural gas discoveries off Cyprus, the whole industry has been in turmoil. If large deposits are stored in front of Famagusta, then certainly in the Aegean. This is also supported by the numerous activities of the Turkish army, which would certainly not lead to a dispute over small, barren rocks, there would be nothing to bring.

In case of Mikonos Poroshenko and his clients were lucky.

On the second day, they found what they were looking for.

3

"Tell me, how stupid do you think we are?", Mayor and Chief Inspector Angelos Nikakis roared into the phone.

His interlocutor was the Greek Prime Minister Antonis Migiakis.

The unconventional tone was that only the Premier, Angelos and his husband Alex knew of a secret in the past of the Prime Minister. For Antonis Migiakis had a Turkish mother and was therefore half Turkish. What would not be a problem in other countries is unthinkable in Greece. In the common history of both countries, it would be more likely that Angela Merkel would head the government in Athens than a half Turkish.

The secret was well guarded but was revealed when the adoption bill emerged in the murder investigation of Karamanlis - with Migiakis' original name and that of his mother.

The commissioner had addressed the prime minister in a private conversation, but assured him that he would keep the secret, because for him the origin of someone was not a criterion for anything. On the contrary: Angelos Nikakis found the matter: funny. And: he had forbidden his spouse Alex to call the PM "Mustafa" at home and Alex stuck to it. However, Angelos had "asked", that funding for Mikonos be considered more benevolent than Migiakis' predecessor.

"Blackmail!", Migiakis said.

"No. A request, 'was Angelos' answer. Migiakis laughed.

"It would attract attention if we favor your community!"

"Oh, there you will find a way. And besides, I promised you never to make it public. And my word of honor is really one! "

What the PM knew.

That the mayor has a personal relationship to the prime minister, had spread quickly over Mikonos. Everyone puzzled over the reasons. The two had a sexual relationship, was one of the rumors.

"Migiakis is over fifty. I already have problems with a 36-year-old man", Angelos said to Alex, laughing and Alex promptly threw the espresso cup in direction of Angelos.

But it was clear to everyone that the apparently private connection - of whatever kind - was more than useful to the island. And everyone was astonished when last fall they began renovating the ring road - actually the only island road - which had been waited for more than 15 years.

The mayor had always grinned, as he was addressed about the unusual speed of realization of projects since he was elected.

"You are no better than all the others who want to get hold of private rails", Alex said. "Everyone on this island is pleased, but not my own husband. It's just that even the straight Premier thinks that ... "

"... you are the best looking and smartest mayor in the country, I know!", added Alex. Their running gag - and they both laughed.

On this day, however, it was loud on the phone.

"What's the name of the ship? 'Ocean Saver'? Antonis, if it were not so serious, I would laugh now because it is so absurd. I'm sure I do not find this vessel in the ship register", Angelos said, still loud.

"Believe me. I have it checked. And please calm down. It's a marine exploration vessel ... "

At that point Angelos got a laugh attack.

"Wonderful. So Texaco and Exxon, and as they all are called, are proving more and more humor. Either you are fooled or ... "

"I'm up to no business. The ship wants to be there for ten days. Ten nautical miles off Mikonos! Far away!"

"When they drill for oil, the broth will be on our beaches after five days. And who is cleaning then? You?"

"There is no talk of oil, my God!"

"Now listen to me. We may be provincial, but we also know that oil or gas is being sought or has been found off Cyprus and throughout the Aegean. Why do you think why the Turks constantly wander among our islands?", Angelos said. "Are they looking for sandy beaches?"

"These are just the usual provocations", Migiakis tried to calm Angelos.

"But one thing must be clear to you too. The state is bankrupt ... "

"... as if I would not know that. Especially as mayor! "

"Yes. If large amounts of gas would be found, purely hypothetically, of course, that could be the way out of the crisis! "

"For you in Athens maybe. But that would be the end for Mikonos or Samos. Do you have a picture of this famous ship?"

"No. But I'll tell the Maritime Ministry to email you one", Migiakis was still trying to appease Angelos.

"If that's what I really believe, then I'll sink it personally!"
"I am sure about that. But do not worry", Migiakis concluded the call.
I know exactly which way the wind is blowing, Angelos Nikakis thought.

4
Ornos, Mikonos

In the house of Angelos and Alex Nikakis the mood was seething. "If only I had never given my blessing to this candidature. Every day, you come home in a bad mood", Alex growled.

'Then we would have a right-wing as mayor, a committed fascist. Would you prefer that?"

"Honestly, yes. The main thing is that I will get my former Angelos back!"

"Do you feel neglected?", Angelos asked irritably.

"If so, that would be pretty unfair. I do everything to please you. And if I'm not allowed to talk to you about my problems, who else? Should I ask the wall? It's my job!"

Maybe being the mayor *and* commissioner is a bit too much, Alex thought.

Alex knew Angelos. A fresh espresso always touched his mind. When he put it on the kitchen table, he said:
"I have nothing to blame you for. Anyway, you'll get along with your marital duties", smirked Alex.
'These are not duties. Otherwise it would only be every Saturday and that's not the case! You're messing me up now! "
"You're welcome. Let us stop. I should have avoided the comment. I know - and that's not a reproach - that you're an adrenaline junkie and there's nothing worse for you than having to sit at home! "
Angelos smiled. Thank goodness, Alex thought.
"You know me. I would become insulting if ... "
"If you would have nothing to do. But not that you stay mayor for 30 years!" You promised …"
"That I stop after two years. That would be in two weeks", Angelos said, laughing.
"But be honest. You enjoy your status as First Lady!"
Promptly flew the dishcloth around Angelos´ ears.
"I've never worn women's clothes and never will", Alex growled.
"No. You are a real man, arkoudaki-mou! How about if you show it to me?"
And Angelos grinned.

"Whenever you call me arkoudaki, I know what's coming!"
So Mr. Mayor and arkoudaki went upstairs.
For an hour the "Ocean Saver" was forgotten.
(arkoudaki= little bear)

5

"He lied to me", Angelos scolded. "Just wait. I will show you, Mustafa!"
Alex laughed.
"Now you say it yourself!"
"Excuse me. What annoys me most is that he thinks I'm stupid! "
"He certainly does not. He knows about your skills. Either he just wants to gain time. Or he was deceived himself!"
"Gain time", Angelos muttered. "You could be right. Thank God I have you!"
"I used to be a commissioner," Alex said.
"You still are. What are you talking about? In every case you are part of the team. Equal rights. And I listen to you! "
Alex laughed.
'That was the lie of the day. When things get hot, you say 'yes' and me 'no'. And I have to be in the end the savior!"
"What you like to be", Angelos answered with this special big grin Alex always feels weak.
"What did you find out now?", Alex asked.

"This 'Ocean Saver' is registered in Panama. Year of construction 2017. But: on the website of the shipyard is no picture of the ship. A hi-tech research vessel, brand-new and definitely a showpiece - and no picture on the company's website. No advertising for the own company? That's more than strange, right? But if the shipyard is involved, they will not say anything! "

"Definitely. How about contacting one of the NGOs, Greenpeace or others? Maybe they know the ship?"

"Compliments, Commissioner Nikakis", Angelos said with a smile.

"Do you mean yourself or me? After all, we both are called Nikakis! "

"You, of course, you fool. That's a good idea. Maybe I'm wrong!"

"I hate to praise you, but with your hunches you are rarely wrong," said Alex.

"Rarely?"

"OK. Never", Alex laughed.

"If anyone will ever hear us talking like that, he would think of me that I am an arrogant asshole! And by the way, incredibly vain! "

"The latter is true!"

"No. I'm just beautiful", Angelos said with a big smile and Alex got a laugh attack.

"But you are my arrogant, vain and hand-some man. And I love you the way you are!" And the vain and handsome man got watery eyes.

That's the way he is, but only I see him that way.

I'm the only one he trusts so completely that he can let himself down, Alex thought.

I am a lucky guy.

"Ok, I call and you look in the internet for more information!" Angelos kissed Alex on the head and went into the living room to make phone calls.

What struck Alex was, that the ship on the photo bore no resemblance to drill ships.

He was on page ten when he noticed something. He searched for a larger version of the recording, found it and then printed it out.

"Angelos! I got it! The ship is not called that way! In truth it is ... "

"... the Subsea 7," Angelos added as he returned to the kitchen. He still held the mobile phone in his hand and looked dumbfounded.

"That's hard to believe," he said.

"If we find it out in our kitchen, then it is not likely that the government or the ministry will not be able to discover this fraud.

Greenpeace says that this ship has been seen twice near Cyprus. Shortly thereafter, the government announced that there were huge gas fields. However, they do not know who the owner is. But it can only be one of the big corporations and there are not so many. A hand full!"

"Look, the pictures are identical too. It just looks very different from a conventional drilling rig ", Alex said.

"And this impudence to call it a biological research vessel. But for this impudence this thing should be sunk!"

"What you wanna do? Order a torpedo from Amazon? "Alex asked.

"I think of something else."

6

Hugh T. Jackson was sitting in his office on the 74th floor of the AEXCOM tower, looking west. Houston, Texas, groaned under the heat. But as usual in the US, the building was cooled down to 18 degrees. So Jackson could enjoy the sunset.

It had been a good day.

The news from the Aegean were very promising. Fields in near Samos, Mikonos and Crete can now be added to the large gas fields that were discovered off the coast of Cyprus. And the AEXCOM was far ahead in the exploration run. It quickly realized that the bribe was insufficient. The decisive factor was and is political pressure of a great extent, until the politicians do what the company wants. Thankfully there was a man in Washington who understands that. Even better: he acts that way. That companies must declare themselves to the government or the judiciary or even be fined for bribery or market agreements - these days were over when the Muslim had to leave the White House, Jackson thought.

He was the typical representative of the White Supremacy ideology. The growing Hispanization of his native country was a thorn in his side, completely disregarding the fact that Texas was always Mexican until it had been conquered by the white Americans militarily.

As with all Supremacy supporters, Jackson had a simple view of the world: white good, everything else bad. USA chosen by God and therefore superior to all others. That the wealth of the United States rests on the exploitation of the rest of the world, on this idea he would not have guessed it in life. Gorgeous times! Trade unions? Gone. Past. Gone are the days when the Emperor, or better: Jackson had to fret about employee representatives. Idiots, although they were mostly white.

Through a direct contact with the US Department of Foreign Affairs Jackson regularly expressed his wishes. Where on whom pressure must be exerted. His final argument was always only one word: Russia. If we do not act, the Russians will strike. Or the Chinese. A simple view on the facts, therefore I prefer simple solutions.

The American ambassador to Nicosia could have obtained a room in the official residence of the Cypriot head of government, that often he appeared there. On behalf of America. On behalf of AEXCOM.

So now it would be Greece's turn. Of course, Jackson did not even know the name of the Greek Prime minister, but Jackson was not interested in unimportant chess figures. He was king and lady in one person.

A major advantage of AEXCOM was, that it had already begun exploration before approval. The establishing of a foundation for maritime-biological research was a milestone in the history of the company. While others still hurry through corridors of ministries, we are already drilling.

The "Subsea 7" was one of the best investments of the last decades. In the next few months, two more ships will be added.

We are faster than the others.

We are Americans.

Faster and better than the Chinese.

Faster and better than the Russians.

Who worried Jackson, however, were the Emiratis. Or more precisely: the Sharjah Petroleum, SP.

7

Mikonos, Ornos

Another ten thousand miles away, someone else had a crazy idea as well. Angelos Nikakis spent two hours on his notebook, almost googling himself to death. And quite analogously, he had scribbled five pages of paper.

"My beauty, you should take a break or you'll get quadratical eyes", Alex said.

"Pooh. You're right. But knowing a little bit about the subject is part of my job", Angelos replied.

"The job of the mayor or the commissioner?" Alex blurted.

'The ingenious connection of the two. How about a double espresso?"

"Always at your service. What is my double Angelos up to? I know this face.

Broad grin means you have a seemingly crazy idea", said Alex.

"Insane? No. Unusual? Yes. How many fishermen with a boat are still here? "

Alex counted briefly.

"I believe four. There were still sixty fishermen in the sixties. "

"Do you know one of the four? Someone who is not afraid? And needs a little money?"

"Yannis. He is a fisherman from the old school. Rough but hearty", Alex said.

"Fishermen should be home at this time, aren´t they?", Angelos asked. "Not exactly my specialty!"

"Not mine too. But he lives in a tiny house on the Embankment! "

"Then we'll go straight to him," Angelos decided. "Then I need Kostas and Giorgios!" Kostas, the helicopter pilot and Giorgios, Angelos' "adlatus" at City Hall!

First Angelos booked Kostas for a flight the next morning.

"Just after sunrise? At that time, you do not even know what your name is", Kostas teased.

He was right. Both named Nikakis were longsleepers. Mr. Mayor had no office hours before twelve.

"Giorgios? You take the next plane to Athens, take a taxi and get there five canisters. Write down the address!"

Giorgios was used to such assignments. It was only a 22 minutes-flight to Athens and Aegean Airlines would take the five canisters on the plane without fee, after all, it was basically *the* regional airline, although it now flies all over Europe.

"Where are the canisters going?", Giorgios asked.

"I will send you a text message!"

"Last question: what kind of shop is that?"

"A wholesaler of event and craft supplies. Cash payment. You will get the money from me. Tomorrow. And thank you, Giorgios! "

"Giorgios is really gold," Alex said.

"Are you telling me now because of what you will be back on TV?", Alex asked.

"When we're at Yannis", Angelos answered.

8

"I should do what? Alex, your husband is crazy,", Yannis said straight out. "Sorry, mayor!" Angelos laughed.

"No problem!"

"Angelos, he's right. You're producing fake news although you're always upset about it!"

"Alex, if one side starts with bad tricks, you can not expect the other side to act correctly. What does it help you to be the moral winner if you lose? And this is about preventing the island and the sea from getting contaminated. That's what the people expect from me", Angelos explained.

"Alex, your, um, um. husband must do anything to protect the sea. It's the only thing we have.

I do not like what happened to this island, but I live in the past. It is about the future of the people here and in such a situation all means are allowed. Ok, except murder! Or?"

It was probably the longest speech Yannis had ever made.

"Everyone is always on your side", Alex growled.

Angelos hugged and kissed Alex. Yannis turned away. He could not cope with the realities of the 21st century.

"So, mayor. I am old and forgetful. Can you give me another ... "

"Naturally. Well. The day after tomorrow you will find 5 canisters in front of the town hall. You take them on the boat. Then you drive to the 'Ocean Saver'. It is exactly 13 nautical miles east. It also dawns already. You drive as close as possible to the ship and tilts the entire contents of the canisters into the sea. Then you send me a text message! "

Yannis looked at Angelos questioningly.

"What is a text message?"

Alex snorted.

"Ok, you have a signal gun?"

Yannis nodded.

"Well. You drive on and after a few minutes you shoot a cartridge. We see it in the helicopter! Anything else unclear?",Angelos asked.

"Yes. What's in the canisters?"

Angelos smiled.

"In the canisters is deco water concentrate. Fifty liters make up 50,000 liters of black water."

Yannis still did not understand.

"We are fabricating the first eco-friendly oil spill in history."

9

At 6:12 am, despite the late twilight, one could see the sparks from the helicopter.

"Over there", Kostas said unnecessarily.

" I can see it", growled Angelos, barely opening his eyes. "And do not yell into the microphone!"

"Ah, Mr. Mayor probably had sex instead of sleeping?"

"Suck me, Kostas!"

"I leave that to Alex. Now we have the ship and a big black spot. Once around?"

"Once high and the second time deeper and then back. I hope I have everything perfectly in the box! "

Kostas laughed.

"Not if you're shaking it like that. Get a grip and let's go. "

Six minutes later, Kostas landed on the kite-surfer beach in Ornos. The whirling sand – Angelos totally felt apart.

Bed. Sleep for two hours. Then produce "Breaking News".

This is what the rudimentary planning looked like.

10

At 10:30 am, Alex went down to the kitchen and pressed the espresso machine button twice. He took the cup into the living room and turned on the TV.

The Breaking News were already on air, on the bottom of the screen, you could read: OILSLICK NEAR MIKONOS - OILSPILL COMES FROM A RESEARCH SHIP - HIDDEN ILLEGAL DRILLING - 100,000 LITERS IN THE SEA. SHIP LEFT THE SCENE.

So Angelos had formulated the message in bed before sleeping and sent it to the TV stations and newspapers with the video file. The Message was also published on the Facebook page of the community Mikonos.

With already 312 comments or better: wild insults to the big multinational companies. Alex was split. On one hand the horror of how easy it is to generate "news". On the other hand, he was somehow proud of Angelos. He had managed, with the help of two men and five canisters, to make THE international headline of the day. The rest was invented by the media.

Out of the 50,000 liters from the original message, TV stations have already made 100.000 litres.

Of course, the 11 o'clock news started with this message and showed the pictures. It was the footage of Angelos' flight.

"Soon we will talk to the mayor of Mikonos, Angelos Nikakis!"

So? Hardly possible, because the mayor was still in a coma. Barely finished, Alex heard Angelos coming down the stairs, still visibly standing next to him, and he immediately disappeared into the kitchen. The hiss of the machine. And a relieved sigh.

Alex had to laugh. Angelos stood at the kitchen table in his retro shorts. Alex felt that his hormone level rose. After two years he still could not get enough.

Angelos sat down next to Alex on the couch. "Morning erection or was that me?" He asked with a grin.

"Stupid question!"

"But you have to wait. In half an hour these idiots call", growled Angelos.

"Great show", Alex said appreciatively.

Angelos smiled.

"But that was not all!"

"What are you doing when the helicopters arrive and your black water is almost gone?"

"Driven by the west wind into the open sea!"

"We have north wind, my beauty!"

"Does not interest anyone. People do not even know the wind direction outside their window", Angelos replied.

"Tomorrow there are new pictures. Rocks soiled with oil, which are cleaned by the fire department!"

"And let me guess: Kostas and his firefighters have tipped half a barrel over the rocks before. Of course, in a place in the Northeast, no men and no beaches! But: when the oil spill moves east, 'into the open sea', how does the oil get to the northeast of the island? ", Alex asked.

"Ah, the commissioner still exists! Special Ocean circulations around Mikonos. Known only to the people here. Who wants to refute that? And again, who should ask? Nobody will believe the shipowners anyway. And in three days everything is forgotten. But the gentlemen had two extremely unpleasant days. "

"Special ocean circulations? Please close the door during the call, otherwise I will laugh out loud! "

The TV was still running. With updated "news": SHIP BELONGS TO THE AMERICAN AEXCOM. IDENTIFICATION SIGNS REMOVED. MARINE STOPS SHIP NEAR SANTORINI.

"You called the navy?"
"Nonsense. The sea police!"
"But they will not find anything besides the name change", Alex replied.
"Doesn´t matter. Now people no longer discuss the oil, but the dizziness. And we know who this 'ocean rescuer' belongs to. Thanks to my colleagues from the television", Angelos laughed.

11

Athens, Villa Maximos

That miserable bastard, thought Prime Minister Antonis Migiakis. A cell phone camera and a few canisters are sufficient for the media world. Modern times.

He was annoyed, but also full of respect for his opponent.

I have to get out of here right now, the PM thought. Before the American ambassador shows up.

I cannot stand it now. He always appears here as if he was the real king of my country, typical for a world power.

Cultureless idiots, Migiakis thought with the superiority of most Europeans.

The Prime Minister left Villa Maximos when his secretary called after him: "Do not forget the appointment with the ambassador of Sharjah!"

Migiakis nodded - and wondered what the sheikh wants from him. He probably will not bring a cheque, he thought. That's a pity.

In Houston, Texas, eleven men had their heads drawn. The thirteenth roared without ceasing. It was the biggest PR disaster in the company´s history. Discretion was always the top priority. And now we are in an unequaled media shitstorm.

"Whoever screwed that up, will not be happy in his life again", Jackson roared.

Like in the primary school one carefully raised his hand.

"WHAT?" Jackson shouted.

"It was not oil, as we know it now," said the brave young man, who would have better kept his mouth shut.

"WHO IS INTERESTED IN DETAILS TODAY? AFTER TWO DAYS MEDIA STAGE? I WANT TO KNOW WHO IS BEHIND ALL THAT! THE EMIRATIS? THE RUSSIANS?"

"Uh, no. It was probably the mayor of Mikonos, who staged this", a second man said with courage.

"A MAYOR ??" Jackson pronounced the word as if it would be a synonym for 'cockroach'.

"Yes. It looks like everything was planned by him alone. The office of the Greek Prime Minister has sent us a short note, it lies on your table.

Everyone in the house knew that Jackson's attention span had exactly the length of half a page. In big letters.

Reluctantly, Jackson took the paper.

He raised an eyebrow.

"A FUCKING FAGGOT FOOLS ME? IN ANCIENT TIMES WE WOULD HAVE CUT OFF HIS TESTICALS. YES. WHEN THE WORLD WAS STILL IN ORDER!"

Jackson was still snorting, but at least he sat down. Usually the sign that the worst choleric attack was over.

"Where is our ship now?"

"In the harbor of Rhodes. Our lawyers say, it will be released tomorrow. However, without a captain. He's being charged with drilling and illegal labeling!"

"If he cannot lead the ship, he should die in this Greek hole. Get a new captain to take over the ship!"

"And what are we going to do with Poroshenko?"

"I TOLD YOU. NOTHING. HE SHOULD GO TO THE DEVIL! "

Jackson leaned back.

"Get me Clarke! Immediately!"

Clarke was Jackson's all-purpose weapon. The "Operation Royals" crossed the line between crazy idea and reality.

12

"Do you have any idea what you did to me, Angelos? The American ambassador hopped around like a jojo ", growled Prime Minister Migiakis.

"Well, then it was worth it. The man is a ... "

"... complete idiot. As if I did not know that, Angelos. But the guy is so outrageous that you would think Greece is American!"

"You lied to me, Antonis!", Angelos said.

"And you created the fake news of the year. Congrats. So don't you dare get morally superior on me. "

"You forget who started. I only reacted!" Migiakis laughed.

"I should have known it. But honestly. At first I was almost hit by the blow and then I laughed loud. One should not mess with you!"

"Just remember that for the future", Angelos suggested.

"How is the mood in Athens?

"What do you think? Don´t you hear the cries of the Greenpeace idiots in front of my villa? Your fake pictures of the oil-smeared coast were impressive. Did you pay the oil yourself?"

"No. The fire department", Angelos answered calmly.

Migiakis laughed out loud.

"Bastard. But I have something else for you!"

"Oh dear. The next attack on my nerves!"

"Certainly. The ambassador of Sharjah was here. The crown princess is coming to you! "

"Crown Princess? There is no female succession to the sheikhs", Angelos stated.

"Ah, the gentleman is reading the yellow press?", mocked Migiakis. "She has the title anyway."

"Aha. And what does she want here? "

"Supposedly a beauty surgery!"

Angelos laughed loudly.

"So a sex and drugs cure! Wonderful! But I refuse to play the nanny for a spoiled royal ..!"

"I have recommended you as our most competent security officer!"
"That's the payback?", Angelos asked.
"But a harmless one. Would you have preferred the Crown Prince? "
"With your permission, Mr. Prime Minister, you are a complete idiot!"

13

"I'm not a nanny, "Angelos growled as both Nikakis´ went to bed.
"Would it be the crown prince ..."
"Now you too? First, I do not even know what the prince looks like. Second, I'm no bodyguard and ... "
"Third, you do not like women," Alex said.
"That's not true. I just do not like them when they are bitchy and loud", Angelos said.
He was what is called a macho gay. No spark feminine. Angelos reacts to drag queens much like a Catholic priest. Although ...
"That annoys me. Why do they always have to be so shrill?"
For Angelos a CSD was an abomination. Point 1 crowds. Point 2 too loud. Point 3 too pink.

Alex called him a "gay hetero". In fact, Angelos had nothing to do with women and had never touched one.

"Why should I? A woman's body is as erotic as a wooden box! "

Alex, on the other hand, was even married once - so with a woman. "That makes every straight gay", he joked always. He had always explained his lack of sexual desire in his marriage with his laziness. When Alex met Angelos, he realized that he missed a lot. And it was made up.

"What does she look like?" Alex asked and Angelos slid the notebook on Alex´ side of the bed.

"She is an oriental beauty," Alex said. Angelos scowled at him.

"Of course not as nice and smart as you", Alex added.

"Toady."

Angelos moved closer to Alex and whispered in his ear: "Do you get a heterosexual fallback? We should check that immediately!"

He gently licked Alex' ear. Five seconds later, the proof of the opposite was visible.

"Well. Calms me", Angelos said, turning away with a grin.

"You cannot let me lie here like this", Alex complained.

"Call Safiye", Angelos growled.

"I'm married to you and not to someone else",
Alex said. "Pleeeease!"
"You want sex with the mayor?"
Angelos laughed.
"And with my husband". Alex added, whose
hormone level was already in the deep red
zone.
An hour later, Alex was physically exhausted,
but in high spirits.
"Happy, arkoudaki-mou?", asked a sweaty
Angelos.
"Oh, yeah!" Arkoudaki was satisfied.

14

Houston

Clarke had learned not to contradict
Jackson or to object. He kept his doubts for
himself. He had to find solutions himself. Plans
have the characteristic that they are often
wasted paper even before the first step.
That's why Clarke worked with corridors and
almost always developed a kind of pedigree.
If step A works, then continue with ...
If A does not work, then continue with ...
That's how it always went. And Clarke was
more than prosperous. Jackson awaited the

execution of his plans. The result counted, not the way there. That was Clarke's thing.

"What about the local police?"

'Two commissioners and a few men at the traffic police! And: the two commissioners are married to each other! "

"A female commissioner?", Jackson asked. Already this exceeded his imagination. As expected, he had not read the dossier.

"No. Both men. Nevertheless married. Not uncommon on Mikonos", Clarke said.

Jackson hated VIP-places like Marbella or Monaco. It is the best not to go on vacation and if so, then at home. In good, old America.

"One of them is also mayor. He got us into this mess. "

"If necessary, you know...", Jackson said.

"More attention? I would advise against that - with all due respect. I have to keep him under observation or even better under control. We should not underestimate him. According to the dossier, he has brought the prime minister into enormous difficulties. Rumors say that the two have made a truce!"

"Meaning, this mayor blackmails Migiapoulos!", Jackson interjected.

"Migiakis. Yes, I think so. Nikakis has for sure an exit plan. And that means that the Greek government cannot and will not help us. The usual procedure with pressure, pressure and again pressure will not work. But I prefer clear fronts anyway. "

"Then watch your butt, Clarke!" Jackson laughed about his own joke.

"What's important is that Washington has to make sure that I'm part of the investigation team. The Emir will certainly ask for help from Washington. Specialists from the FBI or CIA, anyway. And I need technology and weapons on site. I have the list here!"

"Consider it as done. When does it start?"

"Well, the Crown Princess will arrive the day after tomorrow. It will happen in the next two days ", Clarke said.

"Not a little short for preparations?" Jackson asked.

"No. It's always the same procedure. Only the location changes. In addition, I know Mikonos! "

"So? Do not say that you were walking around with suspenders!"

Jackson whinnied again.

You're a primitive asshole, Clarke thought.

A well paying asshole.

But Clarke had no illusions. Should he get into trouble, Jackson would not move a finger.

The captain of "Subsea 7" had already experienced the "Jackson method".

Before entering the top floor of the AEXCOM tower, every visitor had to hand over the cell phone and walk through a detector.

However, what the detector could not detect, was the small 8mm bug of Russian production.

My insurance, Clarke thought, and took a taxi to the airport.

Houston. Atlanta. Athens. Mikonos.

First class, because Clarke needed the time to prepare.

For the fifth time he read the gossip, according to which the Princess of Sharjah is rumored to be undergoing a plastic surgery on Mikonos.

Rumors.

Hopefully no one in the palace will read the article, otherwise the Emir will ban the trip, Clarke thought.

15

Mikonos

"NO. Under no circumstances you can go to the airport dressed this way", Alex said firmly. Angelos looked puzzled. Jeans and white muscle shirt. As always.

"Since when do you no longer like that? Should I be worried?"

"Idiot. I like that best, but for a 'Royal Highness' it's a bit too casual. "

"Royal Highness? I thought, these times are over?"

"That means you did not read the mail from the protocol service", Alex sighed.

"No. Peck on the right and left are probably not appropriate?", Angelos asked looking innocently.

"It's a crown princess and not a prince", Alex teased.

"Now you are the idiot. So: no kisses, no hello, Safiye! 'And no arm-around-the-shoulder. How about black pants and a jacket? But you can forget a tie!"

"Now we're getting closer!"

Angelos took off his jeans again and heard Alex growl.

"Holy God, Alex. It is not even ten hours ago. I have a sex monster as husband", Angelos said laughing.

"Would you prefer that I yawn instead of growl?"

"Would anyone yawn at this sight?", Angelos asked, pulling down his shorts slowly.

I need to get out of here right now, Alex thought, turning and slamming against the doorframe. Swaying, he went to the bathroom.

"Alex? You're not going to masturbate?", Angelos asked, laughing. "Or would you prefer me to come in? Ten minutes left. That might be ... "

The door opened. One hand grabbed
Angelos' shirt and pulled him inside.
"But do not complain if you have stains on
your pants afterwards!"

16

Mikonos, airport

The Learjet has taken the parking position
and the engines were shut down. Alex was
nervous because in a few moments the stairs
would be extended. Angelos was still in the
Airport bathroom, trying to dry the stain on his
T-shirt. Thankfully, there were toilets with hand
dryers. My fault, Alex thought, wondering that
he could not control his urges at all.
The door opened and first two men came
out, who could have signs with the word "bat"
on their foreheads. And then she came. A
beauty with bright green eyes in a black
cocktail dress.
The top ayatollah in the country would get a
stroke. A scene like from a photo shooting,
the hair fluttering through the wind.
"Welcome to Mikonos, Royal Highness," Alex
said, bowing slightly.

"Thank you very much. Are you the mayor and my chief protector? ", asked Safiye.
Alex shook his head.
"No, that's him!" And pointed to Angelos, who ran to the plane.
"THAT is the mayor? Do all men here look like this? ", Safiye asked.
Angelos shook her hand, a little out of breath.
"Alex has already welcomed you.
May I introduce, Alexandros Nikakis. And I'm Angelos Nikakis!"
"I am a bit confused. You do not look like brothers!", Safiye said.
"Uh, we are not brothers, we are married.
Alex is my husband", Angelos replied.
For a moment Safiye looked disturbed, but she understood quickly.

"Oh. I'm embarrassed now. But I think I will feel very comfortable here. May I invite the gentlemen to dinner? If I have to spend one more day with these idiots on my side,
I will jump off the cliffs. I want to know everything about you both, of course, only if you want to tell me!"
"We gladly accept your invitation", Angelos said. "Dinner with security!"
Safiye smiled.
"See you at ten in the 'Mykonos Villas' in Kalafati!"
"One more short question. When and where is your, well, surgery?", Alex asked.

"What surgery?", Safiye asked and laughed.
"But do not tell the cabinets. And it could be that I need some insider tips from you!"
Angelos laughed.
"Will be done. See you later!"
As they walked back to their car, Angelos heard the Crown Princess saying: "I must call my brother!"
Alex had heard it, too.
"What did she mean by that?"
"I have not the slightest idea!"

17

Clarke was - despite first class - after 18 hours of flight completely out of order. The only thing he realized when he arrived at Mikonos airport were the pleasant temperatures of 25 degrees. A good sign. He had performed enough operations in the blazing heat or in freezing cold to know that moderate temperatures are helpful. Especially in the heat, thinking is difficult.
He drove his rental car, the inevitable black SUV, to his hotel, the Solymar in Kalo Livadi. The beach was less frequented and had two other advantages: there were two access roads and it was just a bay away from Kalafati, where the princess stayed. Although

Clarke could have reserved a house in the "Villas Mykonos", at a horrendous price, it would be too noticeable, since the number of guests was very small. There were only eight luxury villas. In addition, there were more CCTV-cameras density in the area, which was higher than in a television studio. Clarke had not decided where to strike yet, but he guessed it would be better to kidnap her outside the Villas.

On the ride or in one of the clubs. Because one thing Clarke knew: the gossip report in the Internet, she was undergoing a beauty surgery, was a f. The princess certainly did not need such things. Unless she needs to have her hymen restored, in Arabia a kind of trophy for the husband. But a feeling told him that she was still untouched. The Emir is known for not leaving his children unobserved for a minute. The bedrooms of the sons and daughters were bugged and equipped with cameras, without the children knowing.

Clarke had hired three fellow combatants he knew from Afghanistan who had experience in kidnapping. And as a kidnapper. Pashtuns, to whom cruelty was not foreign. In western clothes and with the appropriate hairstyle, they went without problems as a Greek by.

And they had a personal motive: Sharjah had supported the forces that had devastated their homeland. All three Pashtuns lost family members.
Clarke smiled. Hate is the best motivation. And the three would make sure that the topic of hymen would no longer arise.

18

Even Mayor Angelos Nikakis was amazed about the luxury in some of the resorts on "his" island.
He knew some of the real expensive and exclusive hotels. Again and again he wondered what rich people thought is nice. But the faces never express happiness.
The "Villas Mykonos" represented an own world. Each house had its own pool, although pool was not the proper name. It was more like a lake landscape with fountains and small bridges. Between blowing silk towels was covered.
Alex did not shut his mouth. That was the most beautiful thing he has ever seen. And Angelos registered Alex's ecstasy with a grin.

"Well, your eyes really shine in the face of so much beauty. I always thought that only applies to me, "Angelos snorted.

"How come some people think you're a show-off?" Alex joked.

"I have not the slightest idea! Ah, Prinzesschen is coming! "

"Please, Your Highness." Not that there is a diplomatic incident! "

"Do not put your shirt on now. This afternoon, you had sex with a tie - that's embarrassing, "Angelos whispered. Right. It was nice anyway.

"Hello," said the princess as she entered the terrace in a glittering red evening gown, lit by dozens of large torches.

"Your Highness ..." Angelos began.

"Oh, we can leave that. If I'm allowed to say Angelos and Alex, I'm Safiye for you, "Safiye anticipated.

"With pleasure. It would have slipped out anyway.

I'm not a royalist! "

Alex rolled his eyes.

"Do you think so? You're wrong. I and my brother would much prefer democracy.

But the rest of my family lives in the past. Everything around her is modern. A grotesque contrast. Alone, how to treat us women. It's only been ten years since we were allowed to ride a bicycle at all, "complained Safiye.

"That's very reasonable," Angelos heard himself say.

"ANGELOS," hissed Alex.

But the princess laughed loudly.

"So, it's true that gays do not like women!"

"No. It was not meant like that. I have nothing against women as long as they do not touch and yell at me, "Angelos replied, laughing.

"I always thought gays are feminine somehow!"

"Look at him. The overpower, "said Alex.

"Do you want a man in a skirt?" Angelos asked back.

"Of course not. But we certainly bore Safiye! "

"No. I think it's delicious. With us there are ...., shut up, nonsense, with us one sees no gays. Although there are of course. Stop. That's not true. I know one and I like him a lot! "

"What happens in Sharjah when ..."

"ANGELOS!"

"Oh, shut up! The Princess wants to know something, the Princess gets an answer. Now I have a question! "

"Pure comedy", Safiye said, laughing.

"To your question: I think, meanwhile, gays are only getting beatings. Although that is still barbaric, of course! "

"Not always", Angelos said, grinning.

"ANGE .. I give it up." Alex resigned.

"Do not forget. Emirati girls have no idea about sexual things", said Safiye.

"Is that so?"

"Let's change the subject. How did you meet? ", Safiye asked.

"I picked him up on the street", Angelos said.

"Are you kidding me? The truth is: I arrested him. I was ..."

"... you are ...", Angelos interrupted.

"... Commissioner and he obviously took drugs. The eyes were glassy", Alex explained.

"But I thought you were a commissioner and mayor", Safiye said to Angelos.

"I am. But at the time, I was only a commissioner from Saloniki, but on holiday, trying to relax a bit on Mikonos!"

The princess was having a good time. At home such conversations would be unthinkable. Especially not with gays.

"And what did you do then, Alex? Did you put him into jail?"

"I should have done that. No, I took him to my home!"

Safiye's laughter grew louder and louder.

"And you were promptly rewarded for that", Angelos said.

"Oh god, I hope the two burps of bodyguards will not hear us!"

"And a week later I granted him the grace to marry!"

"Are you kidding me? This is miles away from the truth. By the way: what kind of steak is that? It tastes fantastic", Alex said.

"Definitely gay Argentinian beef, hand-raised with milk," Angelos replied.

Now Safiye's laughter was heard all the way to the beach.

"Safiye, what does your program look like? I must ask because we are responsible for your security. And Mikonos is not completely safe!"

"My program? Freedom! Dancing! Drugs! Everything that I cannot do at home. And probably will never do again, because my father already plans my wedding.
I want to do all the things that other girls or women can do all their life! "
Safiye became sad.
"Since I'm married, I cannot do anything anymore", Angelos tried to raise Safiye's mood again. He succeeded.
"Impudence", Alex growled.
"No, no. I'm happy with my arkoudaki! ".
Angelos fondles Alex' head. "Besides, he gets an erection just because of this. Ah, goosebumps!"
"What does 'arkoudaki' mean?", Safiye asked...
"Little bear. He is my bear! "
"Does he growl?", Safiye asked.
"Yes, especially when he's horny. Oh sorry!"
"I am sorry. The three glasses of wine made him drunken", Alex said.
"Back to the topic. It does not make much sense to take the burdocks with you ... "

"Under no circumstances. The two are walking cameras with built-in bugs", Safiye said.

"Then we have no choice but to organize the tour ourselves. If my older man is not too tired!" Angelos patted Alex on the shoulder.

"Clear. You're the eternal beauty and I am the old man ", Alex growled.

"Relax, my beloved husband. I'm thirty and Alex is 36 ", Angelos said.

"You two are really cute. If you go out with me, nothing can happen to me AND I'm having fun! "

"How do we get rid of the burdocks?"

Safiye pulled out her phone, spoke normally and then got loud. The last word sounded like a "Basta"!

Of course, Angelos and Alex understood nothing. The dialogue would have amused them: "I'm going to town with the two commissioners. You do not need to come with me, I'll be protected! "

"Alone with two men? I am sure the Emir will not be amused... "

"The two commissioners are gay and married!"

"What does 'gay' mean?"

Their previous bodyguards were already more than underexposed, but that's why they are chosen. Ignorant, confined and blindly following orders. Most of them are from the desert.

"Gay means 'man loves man'."
Silence.
"No. Nobody can get pregnant. Allah, help
me. They are not interested in women!! It is
not dangerous at all!"

So Alex, Angelos and the princess went off to
plunge into the nightlife of Mikonos.
It would be the last carefree hours in the life
of Princess Safiye.

19

Alex was sitting at the bar in the "Tropicana"
on Paradise Beach, completely exhausted.
Despite the ear plugs, which always lay in the
car, but rather intended for helicopter flights,
his drummings shook. How can you stand it,
he wondered, as the house-beat grew even
louder.
The princess, however, was unstoppable. It
was already the second club. Previously Alex
had to endure the "Scorpio's".
"Please. Can´t you go to Tropicana alone?",
Alex implored Angelos.
"No. You always complain that I do not
involve you and that we are a team. Then we

are also a team, when it gets unpleasant. Do you think I enjoy that?", Angelos answered.
Yeah, you're right, Alex thought. But it was worth trying.
Angelos danced with the princess, who apparently did not know the word fatigue. But she was 19 and "hungry". Completely understandable.
"Now I'm running out of air, too," Angelos complaint as he sat down next to Alex.
"If she thinks I'll keep on doing this for a few more days, she'll be wrong. We showed our good will! "
"But she does not look like she's going to get tired," Alex wailed.
"Oh, just wait a while", Angelos said, pulling a joint from the breast pocket of his sweaty white shirt. "I hope it is not too wet!"
"Where the hell did you get that?"
"Oh, I always have a few in the office. That's how a meeting that makes you cry turns into fun!"
Alex laughed.
'The top policeman has joints in the office. You're unbelievable!"
"As mayor, you have two options: drugs or stroke", Angelos stated.
"So, and now little Princess goes smoking with me on the beach. I bet it does not take 30 minutes and she gets tired! "
It took twenty minutes.

Then Angelos came back and had to hold Safiye, otherwise she would have fallen.

"God, I'm grateful to you", Alex said.

"Desist to show me your gratitude. I just want to sleep! "

Alex wanted to laugh, but sex was unthinkable.

The two bodyguards looked less than pleased when Alex and Angelos led Safiye to the villa.

But if the gentlemen Nikakis felt this day as an imposition: it was nothing compared to the terror of the following day.

20

Cannabis at a late hour causes THC to waft in the brain even in the early morning. And so, Princess Safiye woke up around 8:00 am and felt like she was on a cloud.

She decided to go jogging to the nearest beach - Kalo Livadi. Her bodyguards followed her in the black car.

She ran up the hill, passing Kalafati Beach and followed the road. She was alone. No one, no car to see. Just before she reached the top, her muscles started to work again in an orderly way, for the first time since last night. The marathon dancing had left its mark.

She left the main road and ran to the left, then right again to jog down the steep hill.

I'll take the car back, she thought, as the pain of the steep incline increased. Safiye was compensated by the view of the sea and the beach to the right.

The road, however, became increasingly miserable. Holes in which whole small cars could disappear. A wrong kick and her ankle would be history. Therefore, she was looking for a way to the banquet. Behind her drove the black car. She had to smile when she heard the bodyguards cursing in the car. The underbody paneling creaked several times. On the right stood a car of the OTE, the Greek telephone company. Always busy - not because of normal phones, because on Mikonos you communicate only by mobile phone. No, OTE was permanently busy because of the internet cable. Everywhere on the island construction works and renovations: so, they have too much orders and not enough employees. In this respect, a vehicle of the OTE is part of every street scene.

"Probably has a flat tire", Safiye thought, because in front of the left front wheel kneeled a man who hold a spanner in his hand and seemed so busy that he did not look up.

As Safiye passed by the car, the doors opened and two men in black overalls and masks jumped out. They lunged at Safiye and tore her to the ground.

As she felt, she saw that the man who supposedly took care of the tire, also wore a mask under his baseball cap. And that the cross-key was not one, but a submachine gun.

He immediately opened the fire on the car, which was not a hundred yards away.

The driver was hit, and the car crashed into a big pothole and stopped. But the driver was still alive.

He opened the door, played a role despite injury and went into firing position.

He fired. Too short. Too long. No wonder, because in between he was hit by three bullets.

The second bodyguard first sought cover behind the slightly sloping car. But it was hit by projectiles.

In the meantime, two of the masked ones pushed the princess into the OTE truck.

The third went into a better shooting position, further out to the banquet.

 He shot and the second bodyguard caught a shot in the upper arm and one in the shoulder. The OTE truck swung violently down the road to the beach, disappeared behind the restaurant "Solymar", shortly afterwards in the parking lot to give full speed. He pulled a huge cloud of dust behind him, because the parking lot was not asphalted. The second bodyguard saw the truck driving uphill again at the end of the bay.

The road leads to the next bay: Elia.

My life is not worth a tinker´s guss, the bodyguard thought. He envied his dead colleague. The Emir will beat me to death because I failed.

He reached for his cell phone, pressed a key and spoke.

Then he took his pistol and shot himself in the head.

It was 8:15 in the morning.

21

Kalo Livadi Beach was deserted at this time. Although the ladies and gentlemen of the upper class had heard the firefight in their villas on the mountainside, they either did not care or had instructions from their security staff to stay in the house.
See if in the firefight someone was injured to help: No, not our business.
No one lived in the two rows of houses along the street where the kidnapping occurred. There were cottages. Only a very exclusive hotel was located about 300 meters away from the action. But even there they decided not to look. Anyone who finds corpses always gets in trouble and why spend a whole day on the police, if you can sit by the pool with cocktails.
So, it was Paul Pandis, one of the waiters in the "Solymar" who drove down the steep street and turned right. Behind a knoll he saw a stationary vehicle, next to the two men lay. They lay in pools of blood. Since he had heard no shots - he lived in Ano Mera - he considered it a traffic accident, even if no second vehicle was visible.
He called the police and reported a traffic accident.

The traffic police needed twenty minutes to Kalo Livadi, which is in the east of the island. But then it only took a minute for the police to realize that, thank God, they were not responsible.

At 9.47 am, they called Commissioner Angelos Nikakis. An hour and thirty-two minutes after the incident.

But one of the bodyguards had made a last call. At 8:16 am, the call arrived at the Embassy of Sharjah. The ambassador was not present currently. The female operator did not know how to judge the call. The princess on Mikonos? Unlikely. In addition, the man spoke in choppy sentences. He was badly injured, but she did not know that.

The ambassador arrived at 9.00 am and listened to the phone call. He knew that Safiye was on Mikonos and immediately called the number of the bodyguards. But the ringing in the pool of blood remained unheard.

The ambassador battled for oneself for five minutes if to inform the palace in Sharjah but decided against it. First put pressure, so that the Emir could see, that the embassy already reacted.

The Ambassador called the Villa Maximos, the official residence of the Greek Prime Minister in Athens. There he received the information that the Prime Minister was in a meeting and did not want to be disturbed, "even if the Acropolis collapsed," as the chief secretary aligned the ambassador. She recommended calling the Ministry of Interior, which was responsible.

There, the ambassador received the information that the interior minister was sitting in the same meeting as the Prime Minister.

The ambassador was furious.

"Stupid cow!"

He decided to drive to Villa Maximos and make trouble there.

"Take a seat in the garden. The air is better than in here! "

"I DO NOT NEED GOOD AIR. OUR PRINCESS HAS BEEN ABOLISHED", he roared.

The lady was angry and said that the meeting takes place at the airport Venizelos in the local conference rooms.

As the chief secretary was a left-over of the former left government, she did not like "Royals" at all, not to mention their antiquated image of women. But the ambassador was annoying her.

She remembered that the Prime Minister knew the mayor of Mikonos well. Several times the prime minister asked her to call Mikonos. But for obvious reasons, Migiakis had told her that she had to keep silent about those calls.

"Try your luck at the airport. I do not call.
Clear statement of the Prime Minister."
It was 9:32.
The ambassador drove to the airport. Rush-
hour in Athens and the new airport was out of
town. Perfect.
Even with his diplomatic passport, it took a
while until the prime minister's security officials
let him through.
He was admitted at 10.12.
At 10:13, Prime Minister Migiakis called
Angelos Nikakis.
He was driving down the steep road to Kalo
Livadi. He had been informed 26 minutes ago
by the police and left home immediately.
He was only a curve away from the scene.
An hour and fifty-eight minutes had passed
since the abduction.

He was upset when he heard that the crime
must have been committed before 8:15.

22

Angelos and Alex got out, took a brief look at the scene. Then Angelos called back the Prime Minister.

"Angelos, this is a diplomatic nightmare. The ambassador is furious. The private secretary of the Emir has announced a call from His Excellency! "

'Then tell the Emir that we were not informed until two hours after the incident. Because the dumb bodyguard calls the embassy but not the police. And even the fine Mr. Ambassador runs around in Athens but does not call the police. Obviously, in Sharjah, corpses always lay on the street for two hours before anything is done! "

Angelos was angry.

'Things you cannot change, you know!" Migiakis replied.

"Please tell the Emir the same sentence", growled Angelos. 'Two hours! This means that they could have left the island by ship. Otherwise we could have blocked the harbor and all beach sections. It could have worked with a roadblock. The Emir should behead his ambassador. But in the end, we are to blame again. Typical Greeks, that's what they will say", "snorted Angelos.

"Do you already know anything?"

"No. Ten meters before I reached the scene you have called. I cannot even tell you how many bodies there are!"

"Two", Alex called from the scene.

"At least the princess is not among them", Migiakis said. "We will certainly have to cooperate with their police, are you aware of this?"

"For sure. Two men of the Sharia Police Department. This will be a great investigation, with two sheiks in tow!"

"It's flashing on the phone. That's definitely the Emir. I'm already sick", moaned Migiakis.

"I'll call you right away!"

"And when should we then investigate the crime scene? And do the forensics? I cannot keep talking to you, the Minister of the Interior or the Emir, Damn! "

The prime minister hung up.

"Asshole!"

Angelos went to Alex and hugged him from behind.

"It's going to be a nightmare", he said.

"That is already one. Six hours ago, we were still in the Tropicana with her. The poor girl. And I'm completely exhausted", Alex replied.

"Me too. Five hours sleep. At least I would like to have a shower! "

"I love it when you smell like sweat", Alex said smiling. At the eyes of the two traffic cops, the Mr. and Mr. Nikakis realized that their conversation next to two dead bodies seemed irreverent.

Angelos went to one of the policemen.

"Ok, Nikos. We must lock the entire beach. Call your cousin. He should block the junction above with a bus.

Same thing on the road between Elia and here, from the top. And in such a way that not even a motorcycle gets through. He will get paid, because that will surely be his first question! "

Nikos smiled. "Get done, boss!"

Back at Alex Angelos said:

"Basics first. Opportunity - Medium - Motive. I think the princess wanted to sweat out the cannabis and was jogging. Here, a vehicle must have been waiting for her, because overtaking is not possible on this road. She passed the car, doors open and shut. The kidnappers opened the fire on the vehicle of the bodyguards. The road is blocked, they could only have taken the road to Elia. If only someone would have called immediately ... "

From Elia it was only one mile over steep serpentines up to the main road.

"Forget it. We would never have arrived in time", Alex argued. "If the kidnappers shot both, how could someone still call? Both have a headshot! "

"One survived, called and then shot himself", Angelos stated.

Alex looked at him questioningly.

"What do you think the Emir would have done to a bodyguard who failed to protect his daughter?"

"The same thing he would do to the one who gave drugs to his daughter", Alex said.

Angelos laughed.

"Motive? The brutality is already noticeable. Two dead people suggest that they are no beginners. Political motives? Is there an opposition? I already know the ambassador's answer. So: money. But: they could have kidnapped every other billionaire here. There are enough here. Why then accept that the status of the princess turns it into a criminal case in which several police and intelligence agencies are involved? Much too dangerous compared to a normal abduction! "

Alex nodded.

"It was targeted against the princess or better: The Emir of Sharjah. But why?"

"Good question. Let's begin. After the tracks, we follow the escape route, maybe we´ll find something. "

"You mean a note saying, 'Hello dear Angelos. Was abducted. Best regards'?"

"Idiot", Angelos growled.

There was shouting from the top of the street, Horn. Then a red-faced man came running down the street. Several times he stumbled because the road went extremely steep downhill.

"HOW DARE YOU?" The man roared.

It was Katsakis, the owner of the "Solymar".
"Lock the whole beach?? That's unacceptable!"
Angelos' eardrums vibrated and he was still suffering from the effects of the party night.
"What you say does not interest me at all... This is a crime scene. The tourists go swimming and eating elsewhere today. Basta!"
"And who will refund me? The mayor?"
Angelos approached the man and hissed:
"If you do not disappear instantly, I'll have three tax inspectors checking your files tomorrow. Then the food monitoring will visit you, followed by the construction supervision. And now: Piss off!"
The man wanted to answer but left it and stamped angrily up the street.
Alex laughed.
"I would like to lay the corpses right in front of the Restaurant entrance", growled Angelos.
"Okay, Alex. We are not spared ...! "
"Plastic overcoat. In this heat!"
'That's the least pain, believe me", Angelos said.

23

Angelos had just slipped on the gloves when the phone hummed. It was Migiakis, the Prime Minister.

"Well, how was it?" Angelos asked mockingly.

"Do not ask so stupid. Fifty years ago, these gentlemen were still shitting into the desert, now they believe they are the rulers of the world. As if we were command recipients. A state the size of a fart", Migiakis said.

"A fart with a lot of money", Angelos countered.

"What does he want? Or better: How can he help us?"

"You will not like it: he insists that two officers of his intelligence service will be involved. Even worse: he wants an FBI hijacking expert to join in!" Migiakis kept the phone away from his ear because he already knew what was coming.

"AN AMERICAN? What the hell do AMIS want here? Emiratis? They are welcome. I understand that. But Americans? "

"Angelos. He is a kidnapping expert. How many kidnappings did you have in your career?"

"At least one," growled Angelos.

"But I insisted that the supervision is your business. We are still in Greece. The Emir accepted. "

"When will all these idiots come?"

'The Emiratis are already on the way, what do you think? With the Learjet of the Emir. And the FBI man happens to be in London!"

Which meant that all of them would sit in our kitchen in the evening, Angelos thought.

"One more thing, Antonis. I need something from you. Twenty men at my disposal. I have to check dozens of possible hiding places. And then two patrol boats, in case the princess is on a boat or should be taken there. And no more Schengen flights from Mikonos, Samos and Santorini. We need passport controls everywhere, and thorough ones. "

"Does it have to be that way? For that I have to ask Brussels for permission, and I do not feel like it!"

"And I do not feel like getting a visit of colleagues from Sharjah and Washington. So., I do what I can. And you keep my back free. Understood, Antonis?"

"Yes. Only one thing I cannot promise you: that the Emir does not appear in person. It's about his daughter! "

"… he did not really care about her, as she told me," Angelos replied.

"Since when do you have personal conversations with women?" Migiakis pointedly asked.

"With your permission, Mr. Prime Minister. You are a complete deed!"

Migiakis laughed.

"One more thing: do not think we can keep that off the media. The story will be public as soon as there is only one more police car on the island."

"The Emir insists on a news blackout!" Migiakis said.

Angelos laughed.

'Then spell him the word 'press freedom'. Is definitely something new for him. Besides, we will need the public! At least from a certain point on! "

24

Two hours earlier

Safiye was laying on the floor of the transporter and was dizzy. In addition, the noise was infernal. The howling of the engine.

And then the permanent vibrations whenever they drive in the next pothole.

She still had not realized what had happened. Only a few minutes earlier she was still full of happiness. The evening may have been the best of her life. Freedom. Safiye had felt free for the first time in her life. Without observation, just do what other girls and women do. And in an accompaniment that was more than pleasant. Safiye liked Angelos and Alex a lot. Funny and nice and: not interested in her. The friendliness was genuine and not a means to the end.

She hoped that the two had noticed that her affection was real too. Then they would not only look for a kidnapping victim, but also for a friend.

Help me!

Then the next thought: who are the men and what do they want? For a moment Safiye thought that maybe her own father ... No, he would not go that far. She did not know much about politics. Are there any political opponents who use me as a lever?

Hardly imaginable. Sharjah was a country with a happy population. Safiye had never heard or seen anything else.

Maybe the Qataris are behind it? They and the Emir were or are spiders. At least since the closure of the borders. But an Arabian royal dynasty that kidnaps a member of another Arab ruling family? No, that was unthinkable.

Safiye prayed to Allah and spoke in her mind
to Angelos and Alex.
Suddenly she felt like a damp sponge
was pressed on the face. Above her a man
with a mask. Seconds later, the princess
dawned.

Clarke drove the car. He let the car drift in
each banked turn, then immediately
accelerated again. The stupid slut could
have jogged to Lia. This road is straight and
flat.
But Pashtun 3 had announced that she had
turned off to the right as seen from the villas.
She could only run to Kalo Livadi. Otherwise,
Clarke and Pashtun would have shifted the
scenario to the eastern bay. Both places
Clarke had visited and checked.
Always have a plan B. That was his motto.
Luckily, the car had enough power. He took
that into account. The road from Elia Beach
up towards Ano Mera was a nightmare. One
180-degree-turn after the other.
Clarke took a deep breath as they reached
the top of the plateau and raced along the
narrow street.
The masks had already been taken off
behind the beach. The wigs and the beard
stayed.
He headed for a neuralgic location. The
intersection of the roads to Kalafati, Elia and
Ano Mera. But there could not be police

there yet. The commissioner lives at the other end of the island in Ornos.

As expected, the intersection was clear and there was no car to see. At 8:15 am, neither tourists nor Greeks are on their way. In addition, the east of the island was not a hot spot. Too far off the tourist trails - means: too far away from the Chora, Mikonos Town. Clarke turned left and drove towards Ano Mera, then leisurely left into a gas station. A former gas station and repair workshop. The car stopped in front of a large hall door. Clarke got out of the car slowly because he didn´t want to attract attention. He drove the car into the hall and closed the gate.

"And now speed, but without any noise!" There was a second vehicle in the hall. The two Pashtuns carried the unconscious princess to the car and opened the trunk. They put Safiye in and closed the lid. The day before, they had drilled two breathing holes in the body of the car.

One of the Pashtuns opened the gate and Clarke drove the car out again.

It did not take 90 seconds for the kidnappers to change the vehicle and continued their hideout.

At the same time, Angelos and Alex were still sleeping.

And the ambassador in Athens did not know anything yet.

Only the telephone operator.

25

"Stop. It´s useless", Angelos said, taking off his gloves. He called the policeman.
"Call two more colleagues. They should wait here until the ambulance has taken away the bodies. Then we'll unlock the detours!"
"There are now only two men left in the police station. Then there would be no one left ", one of the policemen answered.
"As if I would not know that", growled Angelos. Since Maria, the head of the department, had gone to a training, there were only four police officers and the two commissioners.
"I hope, nobody's going to run into a business or bank", Alex said to Angelos.
"Now we follow the escape route. Will you please take the laser gauge with you?"
"I do not understand why, but...", Alex replied.
The road to the beach used to run between the beach and the restaurant. The owner had complained for years that guests from the beach could not go straight to his restaurant.
"I understand. You could put the road behind the 'Solymar'. But only one would have the benefit and that would be you. The general public has nothing of it. You have to pay the

construction of the street yourself. You get the approval from me within a day", said Angelos a year ago. Three months later, the new road was finished. The old one became a cactus garden.

"Nicely done", said Alex.

"Definitely. And the city did not have to pay anything. He was too stingy to concretize or asphalt the parking lot. Thank God. So maybe we will still find traces. There was no car here since the closure. Probably not before either. Much too early for tourists or delivery vehicles!"

The parking lot consisted of scree and dust. Typically, Alex thought. Beach and restaurant - the owners spend money on that. How the area around looks, that is not of any interest. Unfortunately, it was the same situation as on the other beaches.

Two months ago, Angelos announced at one of the hotel association's dreaded meetings that the community would cancel all leases unless plans were submitted - within six months - to provide a visually more appealing design of the areas around a beach – and the parking lots. The reaction of the gentlemen - women were none - was predictable. From 'blackmail' to 'dictatorship', the range of comments was sufficient. Today, however, Angelos was glad that the parking lot and the adjoining road to the neighboring bay had not been changed. The dust was so fine that you could clearly see car- and footprints.

Angelos pointed on tire marks.

"That's the track of the escape vehicle!"

"Nice. What does that help us? "

"Give me the laser measuring device", Angelos said.

It took a while until he muttered "205" and then reached for his cell phone.

"Giorgios? You're a cop right now!"

Angelos' adlatus in the town hall understood quickly and asked few questions. And Giorgios was delighted with the temporary transfer, because he wanted to switch to the police for some time, even though all - administration and police - are housed in one building.

"Giorgios, you have to check the track width of vans on the internet, manufacturers or better car rental companies. They have a lot of technical data on their websites."

"But there are hundreds," protested Giorgios.

"Oh, nonsense. Most manufacturers have one or two vans. In different lengths, but the track width is the same. I need the transporter with track width 205 cm. If you have it, call all car rentals.

In case of a hit, you go there personally, and they should make you copies of everything. And you must talk to the employee who talked to the customer. Appearance of the customer, especially characteristics that cannot be changed.

Scars, tattoos. If you have something, call. We are going to Ornos now to check the cameras!"

"Alright, boss!"

When Angelos ended the conversation, Alex said:

"And if they brought the vehicle to Mikonos?"

"I do not think so. They would be seen on all cameras in the harbor. Of course, I'm not sure. But do you have a different approach?"

"No. How could the kidnappers know that Safiye wanted to go jogging? And how did they get to the scene so fast?"

"That's why I said that we go to Ornos to check the cameras. They had to have a man on the spot. And the abduction vehicle must have been standing nearby because they did not know if the princess would run to the left or right. Means, if Safiye left shortly after 8 o'clock, a man must have stood in front of the villas for a long time - and he would have to be seen on the cameras on the beach or on the street" Angelos said.

"Your CCTV-attack has its merits", Alex answered, still believing that Angelos' decision to patch up the island with cameras was not only a little bit exaggerated.

"It makes our work a lot easier. And the tourists feel safer", Angelos argued. And indeed, in the following months, the number of small thefts in the old town went down by 80 percent. Because with quick review of the images it was still enough time to seize the culprit at the port or airport. There were no thieves from Mikonos itself. They would be identifiable immediately.

So, they were always foreigners. But they cannot escape from an island.

"Then we would still have the flight. After reaching the plateau, there are five ways to turn off and there are no cameras. But if they stayed on the main street, then they would have to be seen at 8.20 on the cameras at the junction near Ano Mera. "

"So, let´s go home to our monitoring center", Alex said with a grin.

"To our kitchen", Angelos corrected.

On the way to their car Angelos' mobile grumbled. Giorgios.

"Boss? It must have been a Peugeot boxer. Only it has a width of 205. And only one company offers it. Alamo. I'm going there right now! "

"Respect. Well done. Please ask if they have cameras in their rooms!"

Angelos was relieved. They had a thread. After all.

No. It was a little thread.

26

The Nikakis kitchen was also a kitchen, at least half of it. The other half consisted of monitors, a sideboard with notebooks and a multiboard. The two commissioners had the equipment of a police station, no, better. So, they had access to the data banks of the State police and Interpol much faster than if the access would be in the town hall. In the heart of the city, without parking. And even if Angelos would no longer be mayor, he would remain a commissioner.

They sat at the kitchen table.
"I'm still completely exhausted. Could not they wait one more day?", Alex complained.
But Angelos felt the kick of adrenaline.
"Come on, first of all the camera tapes of this morning in front of the villas."
On the screen there was a person who stood on the street at 07.30 am, at the wall near the beach. But the man had no head. In its place was a white spot.
"What the hell ...", Alex started.
The following pictures did not show anything either. But they could see that the man telephoned at 8:03.
And then disappeared. Previously, the princess had left the villa. She was clearly visible.

Angelos groaned.

"The Alpha Bank in Piraeus", he said disappointed.

"What do you say?"

"A year ago. A bank robbery in Piraeus. And on the camera pictures were only white spots.

When the robbers were caught a week later, T-shirts were found in their apartment, with LED lights sewn into the collar. Not visible with the eye, But the cameras reacted to the lights with glare effects. The result: these white spots. Only the brand-new generation of cameras can handle it, but not older models!"

"And those on our island are all older?"

"Yes. The ones installed before me anyway. And when I got the new ones, they had the year of construction 2016. Two years before Piraeus. We could not have afforded the new ones either. Not in that quantity."

"It was not a reproach, Sweetie", Alex soothed.

"Then the cameras from the junction will also deliver only white spots instead of heads". moaned Angelos.

"FUCK! But at least we know that the hiding place cannot be on the left side of the plateau, otherwise they would have turned off the main road. So, let's take a look at the intersection!"

And indeed. The screen showed 08.16 am:

Junction Elia / Kalafati / Ano Mera.
A Peugeot boxer turning left towards Ano
Mera. With white heads.
"Well. That means they could have gone
anywhere except Kalafati, Elia and
everywhere on the left side of the plateau.
Means: 90% of the island remains. "

Angelos did not look pleased. But that
changed within a minute.
Giorgios.
"I just come from Alamo. Three days ago, at
3.32 in the afternoon. A Peugeot boxer. The
tenant paid cash, no return date.
The name is David Allister, Englishman. "
"Definitely a wrong name. But still: well done,
Giorgios. If the Emir gets his daughter back,
he will reward everyone who contributed.
And I will not forget you! "
"That's not why I do it!" Giorgios even seemed
a little offended.
"I know that. Unfortunately, the police work
continues. We need to prepare for the
meeting with the Emiratis and the FBI dork.
That's why you must do the following: Hm, at
3:32 pm at Alamo. Then he could have
booked only for the two flights: Condor from
Munich or BA from London. Passenger Lists,
Giorgios!"
"Oh, boss, I forgot something else: I have a
picture of the man. Alamo has a camera in
the interior! "

Angelos was speechless. The man will certainly have a different name and was disguised, but now it was clearly a thread, he thought.
Rather more.

27

There was no time to think. The phone growled. The Prime Minister.
"Permanent line to Athens?", Alex teased.
"What's up?" Angelos growled.
"Do you already know anything? A scrap of information? The Emir calls again in an hour!"
"Tell him, if he does not stop annoying, I'll wring his neck personally - of course after the liberation of his daughter.
"Very funny. I'm just trying to take off pressure on you!"
"You want information? So, write down: We identified one hijacker. The Car: a Peugeot boxer, rented. The name of the boss is David Allister, landed three days ago. We even have a picture of him", Angelos said.
"Thank God."
"You better thank me", Angelos said.
The PM laughed.

"Then I have something to present to the Emir. He will see that we work fast and efficiently. It's been half a day since. Good job, Angelos! "

'Teamwork. The problem is: the name is false, and we do not have any results. The face is not in the database, neither at Interpol nor at Europol. Maybe the Lord of the FBI can scour his clientele. But I have no idea about the whereabout of the princess. Another thing: the whole story comes to the public automatically within the next two days. If not, the kidnappers do it themselves. But you and the Emir, you must wait another 48 hours. Twenty TV teams who then identify or even search on their own will not make the job any easier!"

"Did not the mayor from time to time shut the port and airport?" Migiakis asked.

"Yes. To stop you crooks. But that was for a few hours. The media mob cannot be stopped!"

"Who of us is the bigger crook, that is the question!"

Angelos laughed.

"OK. We are both crooks. But I have noble motives!"

Migiakis laughed loudly.

"Modest as always. Oh yes, there is another agent, but from our secret service, coming to Mikonos!"

"I BEG YOUR PARDON?"

"Blood pressure down, Angelos. I told Kyriakos to send your friend. "
"Nikos? That's OK. He could really be a help!"
"Do you see? First listen, then shout. And now back to work! "

28

The conversation about confidentiality was obsolete thirty minutes later.
On Instagram appeared a post with a picture showing the shot-up vehicle and the two bodies. The site must have been one of the villas on the hillside of Kalo Livadi.
It was on the account of "kaloqueen". And as one of the "Villas" cleaners had blabbered, the news spread that the princess had disappeared. Although all housekeeping ladies were dismissed, it was already too late. With a little help of the cleaning lady in one of the villas up on the slope, the news was scattered and one of the bored ladies in the rich quarter combined - rightly - that both cases were related.
And that is exactly what "kaloqueen" wrote in her post.

"She saw it and called neither police nor ambulance. What's wrong with them? I swear I'll find that stupid bitch", Angelos scolded.
"And then? The fine will be paid out of her husband's petty cash", Alex said.
"Do not worry. I catch her with some trick at a point that really hits her!"
"Ah. For example, at the hairdresser. Instead of shampoo loo cleaner?", Alex replied.
"My love. That's an excellent idea. I will remember that!"
"How long do you think it takes until the BREAKING NEWS on CNN?"
"More likely on Al-Jazeera. 30 minutes?", Angelos growled.
It took 38 minutes.
Ten minutes later, Giorgios called.
"Boss. Journalists keep calling and they want ... "
"I know what they want. Just pull out the plugs and go home. We do not say anything. For what do we have a government?", Angelos asked, grinning.
"And if Migiakis calls?" Alex asked.
"Tell him: I play hide and seek with a princess!"

Angelos looked around the kitchen.
"Is there enough room for our coffee party?"
"I know, I am now the philistine again, but be reasonably nice to the Emiratis and the Ami. We will need them. And you do not want hourly calls from Migiakis!"

Angelos looked indignant.
"I am ALWAYS nice" - and had to laugh himself.
"So: the two of us, two Emiratis, one Ami and Nikos. In total six. So, two more chairs. Is there anything else?"
"No. Great, I would add Giorgios. He was a great help to us! "
"You're right. Ok, seven! "

29

Safiye looked around. One minute ago, she was allowed to remove the hood. After the stupefaction, she had been given the opaque cap.
She sat on an old mattress stained and leaned against the yellowed wall.
She tried to sort her thoughts. Her whole body ached. Did they beat me? Or did the bruises come from the fast-paced ride where she hit her head on the ground several times?
There were two buckets in the corner. One as a toilet, in the other was brackish water.
Only then she realized that the room had no window. Only in one corner was a small barred opening, far too small to pass through.

Until now she was under adrenaline, but now she was exhausted. The evening before. Was it really yesterday? She had been so happy. With the exhaustion came despair.
Why I'm here? For how long?
There was a knock on the door three times. The sign for her to put on the hood. If she will be forgot it only once, it would be her end, the kidnappers told her clearly.
She heard footsteps. Suddenly she got a terrible blow in the face. She was completely stunned when she noticed someone was grabbing her and turning her over.
She felt the breath of a man pulling her leggings down.
"Your Royal Highness will now lose both hymens", the voice said mockingly.
Why two, Safiye thought.
Three seconds later, she knew it.
And screamed.

30

Ornos

the "coffee-party" as Angelos called it, had gathered in the kitchen booth. The greeting of the two Emiratis was formal, Tom Wolfe, the American was tall, with brush cut. Former

marine and / or mercenary, Alex thought.
Heartily like always the arrival of Nikos from
the secret service. They knew each other
since an EYP-mission fifteen months ago. At
the end, Nikos had "forgotten" a lot of
equipment and installed the access to
Interpol and, to a limited extent, to the data
banks of the secret service.
Since Nikos was heterosexual, Alex did not
consider him a competitor.
"Gentlemen, let's start. Safiye was ... "
Angelos did not get any further.
"It's called, Royal Highness," one of the
Emiratis interjected.
"For your information: The princess calls us
Angelos and Alex – and we call her Safiye.
End of discussion!"
That starts off well, Angelos thought.
He gave a brief outline of the incident.
"The vehicle is identified, but not found yet.
The hatched area shows where the hiding
place cannot be, otherwise they would have
left the main road, which they didn´t!"
"There's a lot left," Wolfe said.
Wise guy.
"We're combing through all sorts of hiding
places and nothing comes through the
harbor and the navy patrols around the
island. However, it may be that they have
already left the island, because the
ambassador did not find it necessary to
contact the police! "

The older Emirati protested.

"His Excellency, the Ambassador is beyond criticism, after all he is ..."

"I suppose the Emir´s fifth nephew. Alright", Angelos growled.

"Can the gentlemen from Sharjah possibly serve us with a motive? Family disputes? Political opposition? "Angelos asked.

Both Emiratis got a gasp.

'The royal family is a role model for all of us. And the people in Sharjah are happy. There is no political opposition. For what?", said the younger Emirati.

"Ah. Sharjah means translated: 'paradise'?", growled Angelos.

"Stop the mess for the royal press. This is a police investigation. Either you make a substantial contribution, or shut up", the American interjected loudly.

"Please continue, Mr. Nikakis!"

'Thanks. We have a face ..."

I know the man, thought Tom Wolfe.

"However, without a hit in facial recognition. Maybe you, Mr. Wolfe, could check your databases!"

"At your command!"

Of command. The man has experience, Angelos thought.

"When do you think the hijackers will contact us?", Angelos asked the expert.

"Not before tomorrow evening. The gentle-men must recover and gather their strength! "

Like us, Angelos thought, feeling leaden fatigue.

"Then it's time to wait. I suggest we also gather our strength. Nikos, you stay here. The others have hotel rooms."

"What? You want to go to bed now? And what about the princess?", the young Emirati revolted.

"You are welcome to search all night. Here are two island maps. Good evening, gentlemen! Tomorrow 1000 ".

Wolfe laughed out loud.

The boy is setting out the markers, he thought.

31

It should not last until the evening before the hijackers called.

The next morning, Giorgios was about to burst. After the news about the kidnapped princess was out, he could at least tell the media that the commissioner would make a statement at 12 pm.

But now the next telephone terror started. Every idiot between Salonika and Heraklion now called the town hall of Mykonos. Freeloaders and idiots.

"So, you kidnapped the princess?
What's her name?"
"Aisha."
"Aha. Thanks. Speak to you soon!"
The next.
"So, you kidnapped the princess?"
"Yes. And I demand 10 million euros. My bank details are ... where is this stupid IBAN?"
One more, thought Giorgios.
"So, you kidnapped the princess?"
"Yes. We kidnapped Safiye in a Peugeot boxer. Terms? Give me the number of the negotiator!"
Giorgios gave the kidnapper the number of Angelos and Alex. The conversation lasted less than thirty seconds.
He had just hung up when the next call came.
"Giorgios? This is Masouras, Ano Mera. I was your teacher! You remember?"
Naturally. And so old that his job description would be now "sitting in front of the house until he dies!
"Of course, I remember. But I am suffocating in work!"
"I know. That's why I'm calling. I noticed something. I live at the junction to Kalafati!"
"Go on, Masouras!"
"The youth. Always in a hurry. Anyway, I was sitting in front of my house yesterday morning. Opposite are the old Texaco petrol station

and Yannis' workshop. Nobody has been there for years and I should know! "
Certainly. You see more than a camera, Giorgios thought.
"Anyway, shortly after eight such a big car drove in front of the hall. A man got out, opened the doors and then went in."
Giorgios knew he did not need to ask about the type of car. Masouras had never owned a car.
"Color?" Giorgios tried.
"Something blue on it."
Alamo. YES!
"Anyway, I noticed the number, I'm inside and I wrote it down. It is …"
It was the boxer they were looking for.
"And then? Did he drive out again? "
"No. And I sat outside for the next three hours!"
"Thank you, Masouras. That was important! "
For that, I forgive you even the three "anyway," Giorgios said to himself.
He immediately phoned Angelos and told him about the call.
And that the kidnappers have his number.

32

Safiye sat huddled in the corner of her prison. She sobbed. Her whole body ached.

And she was bleeding. On the thighs: blood. And on the anus. She couldn´t see it, but the Pashtun had maltreated her for an hour. With permission from Clarke.

But there was at least one more Pashtun here in hiding. No, one rape more, she would not survive. She looked around, but there was nothing that could be used as a weapon. Safiye means "the pure". Well, that was yesterday. Officially.

But it was not her first rape.

When she was 14, she was abused by her own uncle. The brother of her father. He had not hit her face so you could not see it. It happened in the palace.

But who could she have said? Her father? His first thought would have been that he won´t find a husband for her anymore. And certainly he would have beaten her, the victim, because the guilty part is always the woman. She presents herself to the man in a provocative way, lewdly dressed and then the offense of the man would be excusable. This is what happens to thousands of women in all Arabian countries. Women's rights as in the Middle Ages, but 5G-network in the last corner of the desert.

She would have liked to entrust herself to her brother. Khalid. But he would have killed his uncle.

Cutting of his genitals cut. But then he would have been unbearable as Crown Prince. He would also break a feud with the uncle's family.

No. I have to protect him, Safiye thought. Now it happened for the second time. And it had been a lot worse. She did not know until now that there was something like rectal sex - and that it is so painful.

Khalid. Help me!

Angelos and Alex. Help me.

Maybe it would have helped her, if she had known that Angelos had been raped too.

It knocked three times. Again, she had to put on the hood.

She was shaking all over.

Please. Not again.

33

Ornos was in a state of excitement. Multiple messages at the same time always cause discussions and sometimes chaos among groups. Unless there is someone who sorts the messages and makes decisions.

"Quiet! Summary: The kidnappers have our phone number. But I do not think they will call before this evening. Wolfe has told us that the calls come mostly in the evening, because the possibilities to react are limited by the darkness. A caller from a telephone booth disappears within seconds. But, Wolfe, unfortunately we have a problem: there are no telephone boxes on Mikonos at all! "

Which was not quite right. There were three, in the center right next to the post office.

"A location will only lead us to the transmission mast, nothing more. A step backwards. Nowadays you can track the phones directly. The mobile phone mast brings us nothing, because in the center sometimes three hundred calls run simultaneously over one mast. Incidentally, the hijackers will not be so stupid as to make phone calls near their hiding place. So, let's focus on WHAT they say. Pay attention to linguistic features, so the accent and specially to sounds from the background. Until then we'll take care of this gas station in Ano Mera! "

Instead of the requested twenty men, Angelos only got twelve. However, there were eight of the OPKE, the special unit of the Ministry of the Interior.

"Of course, there are no blueprints", Angelos stated.

"Excuse me?" Wolfe asked.

"Yes, yes, I know. Backward, sloppy. But that does not help us now. I turned the camera at the junction. According the pictures I made a small drawing!"

Angelos went to the flipchart.

"In front there are the two double doors. Above a ventilation shaft on the flat roof. Behind a door. A local resident has cleared, on my request, any obstacles on the ways behind the garage.

Obstacles were the waist-high walls, typical for Mikonos. These were not boundary walls, as tourists often suspect, but protective walls against the wind, which otherwise would have blown away the thin layer of fertile soil into the sea. Since they were often only cairns due to the winds and their age, they posed a risk.

"Lakis, I planned it that way. An attack during the day. They probably expect it less than at night. The halls are hot and stuffy in the afternoon. You cannot open the wing doors. Hopefully they will be less attentive due to the heat.

Mock attack from the front with stun grenades. Actual attack from behind. Blow up the door. At the same time attack on the skylight. However, without helicopters, that would be too noticeable, even if there are helicopters flying all day: the hijackers do not know that. Let´s just use the good old ladder!"

Lakis was the operational head of the OPKE. "Road closure?"

"Busses sideways, here, here and here," Angelos replied, pointing to the three spots on the map.

"With the attack by day you are certainly right. The busses should be brought into position a minute before, otherwise the hijackers will notice that it is so quiet. You suspect the princess under the lift, right?"

"Yes, or in the office room. But it has a window!"

"Rather unlikely. So, the shaft of the lift would be more appropriate. Over the shafts, old workshops often have massive beams or boards. She would be relatively protected from bullets there!"

Angelos' last sentence visibly calmed the two Emiratis.

"Item reference as shown here on the 1550 plan. Access 1600. Objections?"

There was none.

"Then I'll now give this stupid press statement", Angelos said, grabbing the fifth espresso of the day.

He had ordered the media to Ornos, in front of his own door. It was simply more practical than doing it in town hall. Neither he nor the trucks of the media could park there. In front of Angelos and Alex's house was a large parking lot.

When Angelos wanted to go to the door, he said: "Alex, come with me!"

"What am I supposed to do out there?"

"Stand beside me. Are you my husband or not? Then everyone should see that!"

And so, the mayor and Alex met the pack.

"Statement without questions. Please do not even try to yell at me. All ready? Well."

"For tactical reasons, I can only post a few details. You know that this is partly the so-called 'culprit knowledge' that is important for our investigation! I therefore ask everyone to share information with us before you publicize it. Always think that a person's life depends on it. It does not matter if this person is a princess or not."

In Athens, the Prime Minister rolled his eyes. The Emir will be thrilled, he thought.

"I got to know the kidnapped person personally and consider her a strong woman. Nevertheless, we will do everything we can to free her as soon as possible. The abduction took place the day before yesterday at 8:15. Although residents watched and even recorded the scene, they felt it was more important to post the photos on Instagram than calling the police!"

Murmur.

"I mean the account of 'kaloqueen'. But since the lady did not call the police, it took a lot of time until we were informed!"

Thank God he does not mention the Emirati Ambassador, the PM thought.

"The behavior of the ambassador of Sharjah was also not helpful. Although he was instantly empowered by one of the injured bodyguards, he did not think of calling the police!"

I'll kill him, Migiakis thought in Athens.

'The kidnappers killed both bodyguards. The kidnappers fled Elia high on the plateau. The kidnappers have not contacted us yet. But they have my phone number. In addition to the local criminal police, the secret service and representatives of the Emirati government are involved in the investigation team. All measures will be decided together. I am the negotiator. To conclude, any information that comes out without our approval can endanger the life of the hostage. Thanks!"

34

At 3.50 pm all units were ready.
In front, four OPKE men should create powerful noise and fog. At the same time, two men will enter the disused workshop from above.
The last two would blow up the backdoor. Angelos would follow from the roof, Alex through the back door. Clarke and the two Emiratis should wait in the neighboring house and prevent a possible escape, which would fail anyway due to the busses which block the roads.
There was a crackle in the neighboring house, where the men were waiting for the job and were still being supplied with coffee by the owner of the house.
"Thanks, Yannis", Angelos said. He went to Clarke, who was not nervous at all.
When asked, he said:
"This is not my first time, Nikakis. Storming hideaways belonged to my program for years. Besides, I only have a supporting role!"
From Ornos all units drove off in longer intervals and different directions.
The media pack was still standing on the parking lot, because they were so close to the action. They thought. If something happens, the task force would certainly be

here. "We'll ride behind", the journalists thought.

The police around the world is struggling with this problem. Mikonos as an island had some advantages. The mayor has control over everything. He can close the airport and port in emergency cases. What needs five stamps on the mainland is almost problem-free in the small, almost closed room of an island, especially as islanders stand together in tricky situations.

So Angelos had to block the airspace at 3.30. He planned the razzia for 4.00, because at this time the last charter planes from Munich would have been landed. He wanted to avoid a detour to Samos. As a reason, the tower told the air traffic control that "we have a computer crash at Mikonos airport". There they only laughed:

'The Nikakis virus again?"

They knew the real reason, but they knew also that Angelos was sparing with this remedy.

With the blocking the helicopters of the TV teams were paralyzed. Alex had suggested that some of the units should depart from the kite surfer beach directly in front of their house: transfer by boat to the harbor. There they could change to vehicles. The media representatives would not be able to follow. "Well done", Clarke said.

At 3.59 all men were on their position around the gas station. The inhabitants of Ano Mera would talk for years about the following events, because normally nothing happens in the second largest municipality of the island except maybe a stolen garden gate.

The grenades and smoke candles produced the necessary spectacle. There were explosions on the roof and at the back door too, and the residents saw - from a distance - black-clad and masked men entering the building - but no shots were fired.

Inside you heard several times "secured".

But there was nothing to secure.

The hall was deserted. Only the Peugeot Boxer stood there.

"Damn it. Masouras said no one left the hall!" Angelos stormed across the street to Masouras´ house.

It turned out the man needed more than two minutes to go to the living room, write down the number, and go back to his bench in front of the house.

"And exactly in these two minutes, the kidnappers drove out with the second car. They were in a hurry", Angelos growled.

"The car will not bring us anything. It is definitely cleaner than a surgery room", Alex said.

Angelos nodded.

"Let's go back. But separated. The hyenas will hear about the setback soon enough."

There was still other bad news. Angelos and Alex' only ally, Nikos of the Secret Service, had to go back to Athens.
Why, was a secret. Clear.
"Now we're still two", Angelos said.

35

"When the kidnappers call, I have to ask them something. I will not name you, although you were there. You do not understand anything now, but promise me, you will not get angry", Angelos told Alex. He laughed.
"A blank cheque?"
"Yes, because it's about two or three seconds. You'll understand", Angelos answered. "Trust me!"
"I always do, don´t I??"
"That's right", Angelos said, kissing Alex.
"You take over the tracking. Does not bring anything, but the rest sees that we do something. "
It took twenty minutes until the kidnappers called. But Angelos did not let them speak.

"Listen. This is Angelos Nikakis speaking. Note the following number. Six-nine-five-one-one-four-three-five.

This is a prepaid phone. Under this number, you will talk only with me. No one else. First, I need a proof, that Safiye is still alive. Ask the princess what we were eating during our dinner. Next call on the new phone! "

Angelos hung up.

The Emiratis freaked out.

"Why did not you let him speak? He could have made his demands and you could have asked him about the exchange modalities. The princess already suffers enough!"

"Nonsense", Angelos said. "First, I want to prevent him from talking to anyone else than me. And you are interested in a sign of life, aren´t you? I do not believe in a quick exchange. He would not be on the telephone long enough, so we will not be able to track him. We cannot close the circle tight enough, but he does not know that. He'll ask the princess now and then get in touch with me again!"

Wolfe found that Nikakis was doing every-thing right. Building up a personal relationship by being the only person, who keeps contact with the kidnappers.

In the hiding place Safiye sat huddled on her dirty mattress. The whole body hurted.

Between her legs she was bleeding. Add to that the bruises that hurt.

It knocked three times, which means: put on the hood.

She heard the door open and then footsteps. Then it was shut off again and it was followed by the knocking signal. Safiye removed the hood and saw a note lying next to her.

"What did you eat on the evening with Angelos Nikakis?"

At last. Finally, it is progressing. And Angelos was obviously the negotiator and not some dork from the Emirati police. She hoped, no, she knew that he likes her and that they have a kind of relationship, even though it was only one evening.

Safiye smiled. For the first time since she was kidnapped.

She wrote on the slip:

GAY ARGENTINIAN BEEF.

36

It took only twenty minutes for Angelos' cell phone to pick up the second call from the kidnappers.

"Gay Argentinian beef, whatever that is!"

"It's the right answer. Listen. The calls should not last longer than 30 seconds, otherwise they'll track you! So, call tomorrow at 11 am, then we talk about demands!"

'Otherwise they'll track you'. He tries to distance himself from the authorities. And generates additional pressure through the tracking. Good tactics, Clarke thought.

This brought a - surprising - result. The conversation was transmitted over a radio mast at Merchias in the far northeast. So, they will not be there, Angelos thought. Of course, we could try to shake off the northeast, but first, we would be too late, and secondly, the kidnappers certainly thought about the place for the call well. And what about getting one kidnapper? If he did not return, they would kill the princess.

"We're protesting against this strategy. The whole affair is so protracted. The Emir will not like that,", one of the Emiratis scolded.

"There is no Emir here on Mikonos", Angelos said with a grin. Wolfe almost roared with laughter.

"Shut up. Nikakis is completely right. The Emir for sure prefers that it takes two days longer and that his daughter is alive!"

Angelos was grateful for the support of the FBI agent.

"Since there's nothing left today, I suggest we meet again tomorrow morning", Angelos said.

And besides, I want sex today, otherwise I cannot think clearly tomorrow.

Alex smiled. He knew that Angelos always gets an energy boost after they had sex. And they would need energy.

"May I invite the Emir of Mikonos to go upstairs?", Alex asked.

"Where is the flying carpet?" Did I already tell you today that I love you?"

Alex shook his head. "No".

"Then I should show it to you", Angelos said.

"What does love have to do with sex?" Alex asked with a grin.

"For me it is a unit. And you know that", Angelos said.

37

In fact, Angelos was fit the next morning. The almost black eyes were shining, the pitch-black hair shone and somehow the muscles seemed to be freshly trained.

Which was true. And Alex felt fine too, though exhausted. The Emir could hardly be stopped, he thought.

In the moment when the other members of the team arrived and drunk their first espressos, the "hijacker cell phone" vibrated.

"Nikakis. Listen. Two million dollars. But in diamonds to a maximum of 1 carat. And the Emir must publicly declare on Al-Jazeera that Sharjah Petrol withdraws from the Mediterranean. The reason: protection of the environment. Then he cannot row back!"

"The diamonds will take time", Angelos answered.

"No problem for the Emir. I'll call again tomorrow. Transfer the day after tomorrow. Until then, the declaration must be made! "

Click.

"Not stupid. Small diamonds are easy to sell, easy to transport and color bags for marking do not work."

In other ransom or in case of a bank robbery, the money will be worthless. In addition, the person who opens the suitcase or the bag also carries markings.

All eliminated, Angelos thought.

"Alex, …"

"Sixty pieces of $ 34,000 each", Alex replied before the question was raised.

Angelos addressed to the two Emiratis.

"Your turn. Obtain the diamonds and tell the Emir to make his speech! "

"The diamonds are not a problem. But the Emir won´t accept a blackmail. He will never make such a promise!"

"Well, I think he will. He does not need the gas fields in the Aegean Sea or the Mediter-

111

ranean. His daughter is hopefully more important to him", Angelos said.

"How can you even doubt...", the older Emirati shouted.

Angelos would have liked to tell the two what their Emir has already done to his daughter – But he didn´t say anything.

"Alex, tracking?"

"Radio mast two, Ano Mera South."

Fuck 4G, cursed Angelos. The transmission towers are miles apart. With 5G it would be different. The distances must be much smaller - which makes it easier for the police. To follow the cell phone signal even without a phone call, of course. It is only safe if the mobile phone owner changes the prepaid card after every call. And uses an older model. The smartphones of the new generation are like a mobile bug.

But here they had to deal with vague data. Angelos went to the map.

"The first call was from Merchias, now Ano Mera - both from the eastern half. Kalafati also fails - the kidnappers could have abducted Safiye right there. Everything above Elia on the left too - otherwise they would have turned left!"

"They could have driven back after the car change", Wolfe contradicted.

"Why then change the car? It was a risk!", Angelos said.

He looked at the map and found that the area in which the hiding place is located, was reduced significantly. Based on the theory that the phone calls did NOT come from Safiye's prison, which was likely.

He went to Alex, who was sitting at the notebook, and leaned down to him:
"Are we going outside for a moment?"
To the others Angelos said: "Small private conversation!"
Alex got up and they went to the beach. Meanwhile Wolfe stood in front of the map and had to agree Angelos. Sure, it still was tens of square kilometers. But within the individual areas there were sometimes only a few buildings, in the northeast, for example. Nevertheless, in the rest were numerous buildings without courtyards or garage nearby, then some shops.
Nikakis is coming closer.
Damn close.

38

"Alex, tell me your opinion. What do you think?", Angelos asked, standing on the kite surfer beach.

"Some things do not fit", Alex said.

"And that would be?"

'The demands do not match. Environmentalists would not want diamonds, and criminals would not care about the environment!"

Angelos nodded.

"Exactly. It makes no sense. Something else?"

'The 'colleagues' are a bit suspect to me. No own ideas. They only criticize. Discussing would be alright. But so far, we could have done everything alone, and better. Well, of course, except the gas station razzia ", said Alex.

"I do not like Wolfe. He praises me conspicuously often. And then his last reaction. He completely ignored the map and even put forward a thesis that is really nonsense. What's that about?" Angelos asked.

"I'm not well. Surely you should make the handover. But if there are things going on here that we know nothing about, you're in danger. You may find it out, the others know that. And that means: they must get rid of you, Angelos. So, forget it. I'll be present at the handover, "Alex said.

"That would be Safiye's death sentence", Angelos countered.
"I know it sounds heartless now. Everything is about a girl you talked to for two hours. It's also about me. The girl puts you in danger. And I do not have any regard for that."
Angelos put his arm around Alex.
"If she dies, that does not mean I'm out of danger!"
Angelos was right.
"Let's try that we three - me, you and Safiye - get away as good as possible, which means: alive! Maybe we'll bring some light into the darkness! "
"We have 48 hours. That's not very much time to resolve a kidnapping case involving several party members, some of whom we do not even know", Alex insisted.
"Arkoudaki-mou, have some confidence in me. No one will take your Emir from you", Angelos said.
"You like the title, right? And when does the Emir abolish democracy on this island?"
"What democracy?", Angelos asked.

39

I think the diamond demand is a feint, a distraction. The cessation of the promotion of gas and oil in the Mediterranean seems to me more the essence of the whole. In order to get money or diamonds, the kidnappers could have grabbed another billionaire. There are enough on this island", Wolfe said and went to the map.

"And one phone call location was in Merchias. What if the kidnappers deliberately telephoned from their hiding place because they suspected that we would automatically exclude this place? At Merchias, is there still this camp of the environment protectors?"

"Yes. Most have disappeared just like the oil spill, but a few are still there", Angelos replied.

"What oil spill?" Wolfe asked with a grin.

"Do you seriously think that some Green-peace boys kidnap the head of state's daughter and then hide in a tent camp? Apart from the fact that Greenpeace would lose all credibility."

"I do not think of Greenpeace, but rather of eco-terrorists, which are undeniable!"

Of course, there are radicals here as well. Such as animal protectors and vegetarians. 'Normal' and 'balanced' are obviously dying words, Angelos thought.

"I certainly will not send a special unit to a peaceful camp", Angelos said.
"That's not what I'm talking about, Nikakis. But nobody knows me. I could look around carefully there. As a journalist", Wolfe said.
At least you're out of the way, Angelos thought and nodded.

Shortly after Wolfe had left the house in Ornos, a thunderstorm started. A media storm.
"Agapi mou! Come here", Alex shouted, sitting at the notebook again.
HANDOVER TOMORROW. POLICE CONFIDENT: "WE WILL GET THE KIDNAPPERS! Read on the website of n-tv, the largest Greek news channel.
Angelos almost hit. The statements were all attributed to him. Fake News. The fact, that the handover should be done the next day was correct. But the kidnappers certainly had not issued a press release.
So, the leak had to be found in the crisis team.
Angelos yelled at the Emiratis - there was no one else to get rid of aggression.
But they looked so embarrassed that Angelos realized: they had nothing to do with it. But what about Wolfe, who was under pressure from the Emir.
"Damn. Twenty helicopters will fly above us. Followed by twenty SUVs! "

"That worries me little. You block the airspace again. But this time, we need agents who will prevent the launch of helicopters if they do not respect the ban. As for the persecution by car, we could fall back on buses and trucks. If the handover will be in the East, then we would need ... "

Alex counted the streets on the map. There were eight. Should it be Foko, Merchias or Kalo Livadi, you could do it with less men. "That's how we will do it. I'm talking to the airport. The eight OPKE men are to lock off the runway. Do you make the call for the busses?"

Alex nodded.

Angelos made espresso, took the cup and sat on the steps in front of their house.

His deduction ritual. Do not disturb, was the motto - Alex knew that.

"Do I command you?" Angelos asked as he returned to the house.

"That's all right. Do not worry. I do everything you want; the main thing is that nothing happens to you", Alex said.

Angelos black eyes shone briefly.

Gratitude. Trust. Love.

Then he said:

"Alex, please look at the account of 'kaloqueen'. Every photo, every post, every comment. Maybe you will find something!"

"Any suspicion?" Alex asked.

"Just a feeling. I think the handover will take place in Kalo Livadi. Everything else should surprise me! "

40

In the early evening Athens answered.
The Villa Maximos.
"I'm watching news and learned that tomorrow is the handover. Would be nice if you would have informed the Prime Minister", Migiakis growled.
"Would like to have. But: someone from the gentlemen whom you have sent, talked to the media. And endangers the life of the princess. It occurred to me that not everyone is interested in Safiye's survival,", Angelos said.
"Who should that be?"
"I don´t know. Particularly helpful were neither the Emiratis nor the FBI agent! "
"Angelos. It may happen anything but a dead princess on one of our islands. The consequences would be devastating", said Migiakis.
"Even more for the princess", Angelos replied ironically.
"No time for jokes!"

"I do not have a good feeling!"

Migiakis knew that Angelos´ predictions often became true. He personally had to experience that.

He sighed.

"As if I would have no other problems", the Prime Minister complained.

"But now listen. Sharjah has called. The Emir holds this speech. Tomorrow at 12 am, as the kidnappers have demanded. In Sharjah they said the image gain could be more worth than the gas and oil fields!"

They might be right.

"Listen. If the hijackers were interested in environmental protection, they would demand a complete drill stop. Also in the Persian Gulf. All over. But they demand a stop only for the Aegean and the Mediterranean? That is absurd. That's why I do not think it saves the life of the princess!"

Migiakis thought. Nikakis was right.

'Then we hope it is all about the diamonds! The simplest reason at all: money!

'Two million dollars? Although they could have grabbed one of the other thousand billionaires. Even more absurd!"

"And what's your solution?" Migiakis asked.

"Solution? Gambling. What choice do I have? And somehow save Safiye. And by the way, me too". Angelos answered.

Migiakis sighed.

"Listen. The next bad news: Sharjah has the diamonds. But they will be brought to Mikonos by the Crown Prince! "
Now Angelos groaned.
"Take care that another Royal will disappear!"
And after a pause, Migiakis continued:
"But at last I have good news:
He looks good!"
"Goofy head!"
"You are getting better. Last time I was an 'idiot'! He lands at 6:00 pm on Mikonos. He is waiting for you in the 'Villas' at 8:00 pm!"
Angelos was getting loud.
"Should I play again the royal entertainer? I may have to save his sister. FUCK!

41

"You stupid asshole", the kidnapper shouted into the phone. "Your princess is dead!"
Angelos took a deep breath.
"First, it's not my princess. Second, I did not publish the information. I stick to the agreement. Tonight I will get the diamonds. And the Emir's declaration will be broadcasted tomorrow at 12 noon. Nothing

has changed. Can we talk to each other in a normal way again?"

Silence.

"And who was it? Must have been someone from your team", said the kidnapper.

"No idea. I will do the handover. Alone. And no one knows where it takes place."

"Well. I'll call tomorrow as soon as I have seen the statement on TV! "

Angelos sighed. He had hoped he could clarify the modalities already today.

"No. You have to report again today. Condition of the Emir. We need a new sign of life. The question is: where did I meet Alex?" Hung up.

Not five minutes later, Wolfe was back from Merchias.

"And?", Angelos asked deliberately bored.

"I'd say it was worth it", Wolfe answered triumphantly, holding up a thin bangle.

"Found in the grass on the parking lot at the cliffs. I think the princess dropped it to give us a hint"

"You seriously believe that the princess was conscious at that time?", Angelos asked.

And that came from a hijacking specialist. Angelos tried to remember. Had the princess worn bangles in the "Villas" that evening? And who the hell is wearing jewelry during jogging? On the other hand, she was probably so stoned that morning that she could have run in panties.

"But the bracelet is not cheap. These are all little diamonds", Wolfe countered.

"Is the princess's jewelry still in the 'Villas'?" Angelos asked the Emiratis

"We have put everything in the hotel safe!"

"Well. I'm with the Crown Prince tonight, then I'll see if the ring suits the other jewelry. "

The bangle was so thin that it is usually not worn alone, so ...

42

Houston

Hugh T. Jackson stood at the window of his tower and was satisfied. The craftspeople were already on the roof and he saw the first lights disappear upwards.

His plan had worked well so far. The kidnapping of the princess had caused an immediate swing of the headlines in the media. That is how you control news, Jackson thought.

The Shitstorm after the "oil spill" near Mikonos had ebbed. No one asked anymore about what happened with the "oil" and where the ship was.

And AEXCOM was finally out of the headlines.

Some sponsors of his foundation had dropped off, but Jackson was not depended on them. The big picture was the important thing for him. Big Business. No doubt, the affair "Subsea 7" damaged AEXCOM's reputation and significantly reduced the chances of exploration and getting production licenses. Just mentioning the name AEXCOM, the screaming starts.

But lamenting was not Jackson's thing. Acting quickly and efficient was his motto.

And so he did what every ship company does after a disaster: just change the name. Old core, new facade.

His second coup, however, would be the ultimate one. A serious rival would be knocked out of the field. At least for the moment, because in business nothing is forever.

And if these idiots prevail with their opinion on the alleged climate change, then Washington would protect the own economy by tariffs. An economic wall. For the USA had become an exporter of fossil fuels, no imports anymore. However, if the Democrats win the next election, he would adapt.

Water. His company would change its policy and focus on the most profitable business of the coming decades: water. Jackson had already begun quietly acquiring water rights in areas that were supposed to be sufficiently rainy. If the climate changes, the owners of water rights would face a fresh infusion of funds.

I will definitely win.

Feeling being the greatest, Jackson listened again to Clarke's last report.

Everything went well. In a few hours the Emir would give his speech. The Emir. Pffft. Twenty years ago, he still shits in the desert and now make you king.

Clarke thought one of them might spit in the soup. This miserable cop who had already gotten him into the "Subsea 7 scandal".

And Jackson had issued a clear order:

To dispose.

At the same time Princess Safiye had to endure the next rape. She had stopped resisting. And it seemed like these animals were losing their fun.

Safiye did not scream anymore.

"Tomorrow is the day", one of the rapists had said.

What did that mean?

Tomorrow I will be free? Or: tomorrow I will die?

When it knocked three times, ten minutes later, she had to put on her hood again. It was still wet, so much had Safiye wept in.

A new note, she thought, and was right.
"How did Angelos meet Alex?"
She took the pencil in her hand and wrote:
"Alex arrested Angelos!"

43

"The man arrested you", said the kidnapper.
He almost spat out the "man". This, and the
slight accent, led Angelos to suspect that the
kidnapper was Arab or even Emirati. But this
does not matter.
And Angelos was wrong. The kidnapper on
the phone was Pashtun.
"Well. The diamonds will come tonight.
Handover? "Angelos summarized shortly.
"14.00. Only you. And nobody follows you. We
will watch you! "
You won´t, Angelos thought.
"You're heading for Ano Mera. You get a call
where to bring the diamonds. Then you drive
on and stop after you entered Ano Mera.
After examining the stones, you will get
another call where you will find the princess.
If I see a helicopter, she is dead. If someone
follows you ... "
"... she's dead. Alright. Is there anything else?"
Silence.

"Let's go outside", Angelos said. And Alex followed him.

"Stop. Nothing happens here without our consent", one of the Emiratis snapped.

"I do not care about your opinion. If you follow me, Safiye is dead. You realize that? And now you excuse us!"

Alex and Angelos went to the beach.

"I would suggest that you follow me with a light aircraft ..."

Alex wanted to protest.

"... but I remember your green face from the helicopter", Angelos laughed and put his arm around Alex.

"SUV fails, bus would be inconspicuous, but too unhandy. OTE?", Alex suggested.

"Telephone company? No. Then they would suspect a mobile monitoring center. How about a Veneti van? They are fast enough! "

Could work. Would be unremarkable, because the confectionery vehicles constantly drive from one branch to the other. You leave the house at 1 pm, take the boat and drive to the harbor. Veneti should park the car there. Key under the seat."

"Before sugar in the tank of the other cars?", Alex asked.

Angelos laughed.

"I'm an open book for you, right?"

"A few pages of that book sometimes surprise me, but otherwise it would be boring", Alex said with a grin.

"You take the Glock with you. And the notebook with the transmitter, just in case you lose me!"

"Angelos, I have a bad feeling. The nonsense with the declaration. I do not believe the story about the bangle. Not for a second. You will not find any other jewelry which will match! "

"I do not believe that either. At least not if the Emiratis do not play their own game! "

"Angelos, I do not want to lose you because of a princess from the desert", Alex growled.

"For emergencies, I have you", Angelos replied, kissing Alex.

"Very comfortable", Alex resigned.

"No. That's boundless trust!"

And Angelos smiled.

Alex's grudge twisted.

I am like wax in his hands.

But I am happy.

44

"I'm upset", Angelos growled.

'The last time you liked it in the 'Villas'. Do not say it's not luxurious there!"

"I'd rather lie in bed with you, arkoudaki", Angelos wailed.

"We can still do that afterwards. And now go to the crown prince. At least: nothing will happen there ", Alex said.
No.
The next hours will change everything. Not only concerning the case.

Angelos drove to Kalafati, parked in front of the "Villas" and passed the torches to the third house.
Of course, he was frisked by two security officers, pretty rough, especially between the legs.
"I'm the mayor and commissioner. And I cannot take *that* gun off", he growled, but the joke went past the gentlemen.
And now the prince. Stocky, over-weighty and arrogant.
But Angelos could have imagined, because even he had to admit that Safiye was a very beautiful woman. Sorry. She still Is. And the Crown Prince was very much like Safiye.
He was what is commonly called a dream prince. Mercilessly beautiful. Angelos' mouth struck a lightning xerostom. He stuttered.
"Uh, Wel ... come on M-mikonos, Your Royal ..."
"Let's leave that. I am Khaled and you must be Angelos. Nice that you took time, despite this terrible kidnapping. But Safiye is strong. I hope she makes hot their hell. Come! Let us eat! "

Khaled wore skintight jeans and a sneaky white linen shirt.

Heavens, Angelos thought.

Within a few minutes, Angelos relaxed and started to enjoy the evening.

The abduction was far away. And the Crown Prince was not only beautiful, and funny too.

"You know, I hope you do not think me callous. On the contrary. My sister and I are more than close. But I am sure that everything will go well tomorrow. I trust you", Khaled said.

Khaled knew what was going on in Angelo's head.

"To put it bluntly, my sister told me about you!"

Angelos looked crestfallen. When could she have told Khaled something? Party, drugs, coma, kidnapping. When could she call her brother?

Khaled laughed.

"You look more than confused!"

"When should Safiye have called you? And why? It was a really nice evening, but ... "

Khaled grabbed his cell phone, wiped it, and then held the phone in Angelos´ direction.

It was a picture of Angelos and Alex from the "Tropicana" when they were kissing.

"Safiye called me at four o'clock in the morning. I was already sleeping and was in my room in Istanbul. She was in high spirits and sounded really happy. You probably cannot imagine what an evening in freedom meant to her. And yet she thought of me and then called me "

Angelos still did not understand what the Crown Prince wanted.

"She told me about all the clubs you visited and that it was the most beautiful evening of her life!"

Khaled briefly lowered his eyes.

"It should then turn into the most terrible morning of her life", he added.

"Anyway, she was very excited. Not only because she was dancing and among normal people. The reason for her call was different. She said, 'I have found the perfect man for you! Nice, smart and funny!'"

Khaled smiled.

"And I have to add she was right!"

45

"Well, I cannot be particularly smart if it takes me so long to understand what this is about", Angelos said, still confused.

"Safiye was looking for grooms?"

Khaled laughed.

"No. But she does not just think about herself. She also wants me to be happy. Which is really difficult in my position. "

"Does anybody know about it other than your sister?" Angelos asked.

"For God's sake, no. Even the men I slept with did not know who they were in bed with. But the problem is that it leaves me increasingly cold because ... "

"… something is missing. I was always annoyed by the constant change game. Every week the partners changed. I just found it disgusting. I preferred to be alone. And then I was lucky enough to meet Alex. It sounds stupid, but sometimes it helps to wait!", Angelos added.

"But the situation is different for me. If my father dies, I will be the Emir and he cannot be gay. At least not publicly. So, I would have to refuse the crown, a resignation due to 'health reasons'. And then go abroad as a privateer", Khaled replied.

"Difficult decision". Angelos said.

"Not at all. That's the plan as soon as I will find the right one! "

Does he really mean me? Jesus, don´t beat around the bush!", Angelos thought.

"May I ask you something?"

Khaled moved his upper body forward, resting his elbows on the table and folding his hands. Then he let his eyes shine.

He knows exactly how it works, Angelos thought.

"Are you happy?"

"Oh yeah. Alex is the man of my dreams. He picked me up when I was really down. He has
rebuilt me. Everything I am today I owe to him. "
"Then you were luckier than me", Khaled said. And before Angelos wanted to say again that Khaled just have to wait, Khaled added: "But tell me, if you're so happy, why do you have goose bumps and why do your eyes shine like headlights?"
That was exactly what Angelos could not explain.

46

"It's a bit chilly. Shall we go inside for the coffee?", Khaled asked.
"Of course,", Angelos heard himself saying, even though the fifty centimeters gap between their faces at the table were a perfect wall. Against what?
The two went past the torches and the blowing silk trains into the interior of the villa. Suddenly Khaled stopped and turned around. They were almost nose to nose when it happened.

Khaled kissed Angelos on the mouth. And Angelos could not or did not want to resist. It was a wild, demanding kiss. Khaled's hands went over Angelos' back and wandered deeper.

What am I doing here, Angelos wondered. As Khaled's hands moved forward, Angelos withdrew and said: "Stop. I am sorry. I cannot!"

Khaled's eyes signaled no disappointment, no anger, but pure desperation.

"I'm sorry if I gave false signals. I ... I was confused and still I am", Angelos said softly. Khaled left the room without a word and Angelos thought he saw tears in Khaled's eyes.

You idiot, Angelos said to himself. Now you hurted two people. But one of them will never hear anything about it. Alex. He would not be glad that I stopped the whole thing and praised him, and every word was true. Alex would just see the kiss and would not understand the dynamics of the situation, the atmosphere and the confusion.

How would I react, Angelos wondered.

I would understand it.

And that was the truth.

Angelos' love for Alex could not be shaken by anything. Even if Alex would kiss someone else, it wouldn´t mean anything.

To resist a beautiful man, especially when taken by surprise, is difficult.

And I was always loyal and true to Alex, even though he had twice accused me of being unfaithful. Alex had apologized, but there were scratches. No, I do not say anything. The kiss did not mean anything to me. Khalid obviously saw it differently and Angelos hoped that Khalid would not show anything in the presence of Alex.
Lovers often do irrational things. Sure, otherwise they would not be in love.
And Khalid felt in love with me, no doubt.
The next few days will be a horror, Angelos thought.
And the crystal ball told the truth.

47

After a few minutes, Khalid came out of the bathroom and forced himself to smile.
"It was a mistake. Sorry", Angelos said.
"Why? I enjoyed it. And if you're honest ... But I'll do it the way you recommended. I'll wait. And wait. Maybe you think about it differently and follow your heart. Because it says yes. You cannot deny it. But I do not want to

harass you and I would never - ever - say something to Alex and destroy your marriage. The important thing now is that you bring Safiye to me safely. I trust you!"

Khaled handed Angelos the bag of diamonds.

Angelos decided to focus only on the liberation of Safiye.

"I try what I can. Something is not quite right here. But what? I only have a few hours left. Not much,", Angelos said almost resignedly. On leaving, Khaled called Angelos from behind:

"Are you going to tell Alex?"

Angelos turned around and hesitated with the answer:

"I don't know."

Angelos drove back to Ornos in a trance. He entered the house, went into the kitchen and threw the bag on the table where the two Emiratis sat.

And he just said to Alex one word: "Beach!" Again, the two went the short distance to the sea.

"What happened, sweetie?"

Angelos sighed.

"The short version? First, the Crown Prince is gay. Second, Safiye probably told him about me before the kidnapping. Third, he has a crush on me. Fourth, he looks damned good!"

That was clearly too much information for Alex at once.

"I have an Arabian prince as opponent? I cannot keep up with him!"

"Do not talk crap, Alex. I love you and that's it. But I'm not an ice block. I feel sorry for him", Angelos replied.

"Did you ...?"

"You want to start again? I have not done anything. He kissed me and I stopped it right away. Nothing more happened."

"If so, why do you look so confused?", Alex asked anxiously.

"I do not know", Angelos replied.

"What I do know is that I love you. Is that enough?", he added.

48

The day of decision began according to the plan. Angelos had told Wolfe that the bangle did not match with Safiye's jewelry - though Angelos had completely forgotten about the bangle. It did not matter anymore. In a few hours, the princess would be free, therefore, the search for their hiding place is unnecessary. The hunt for the perpetrators is now secondary", Angelos stated.

Meanwhile Alex left the house through the backdoor and ran to the boat on the beach heading to the harbor.

He was sick. It was not just the usual fear for Angelos life that struck him on the stomach, but also the confusion about the events of yesterday. Did Angelos kiss Khaled? Had he taken Angelos by surprise? And what did "stopped in a timely manner" mean? Where did Khaled have his hands? Just the idea that the Prince had touched Angelos' body, caused high blood pressure.

Trust him. He never betrayed you, Alex tried to calm himself down.

Angelos was not as focused as he should have been facing the upcoming events. He drove remotely in the direction of Ano Mera, a bag full of diamonds on the passenger seat.

Just as he drove into the first tight turn, the phone was buzzing. Angelos cursed.

He heard only one sentence.

"Throw the diamonds out of the right window. Now!"

Silence.

Angelos followed the instruction. No one was visible, but behind the stone parapet it went downhill steeply. They are probably waiting down in the valley and then want to flee to Ftelia.

Shut up, Angelos thought. The Emir has enough diamonds. The most important thing for Angelos was, that - without exception - ALL will piss off his island.

But do I want the Crown Prince to go as well? Angelos had to save the princess, but he still thought about the evening before.

He was angry that Alex wanted to ask if anything had happened. On the other hand, Alex is also confused. So am I, Angelos thought.

He parked the car on the outskirts of Ano Mera and waited. Behind closed doors he spoke into the microphone.

"Alex? Where are you?"

"I stopped in front of the 'Veneti Bakery' for better camouflage. Some asshole parked in the second row and I cannot get out!"

Angelos could have laughed. So much about plans.

"Do not panic, arkoudaki! Take any other car. Just show your Glock to the driver. "

"Prankster!"

Again, the mobile grumbled. That went fast, Angelos thought.

"Turn left, then straight ahead, wait in front of 'Myconian Brothers'."

Angelos drove the 500 meters and stopped in front of the pension. Into the micro, he said only two words:

"Myconian Brothers!"

"Understood. Be careful. I need another minute", Alex replied.

Again, the mobile grumbled.

"Get out, go around the inn, then straight ahead. On the left, the house with the big bougainvillea bush! "

Angelos got out of the car and walked around the guesthouse.

The house was abandoned.

He went to the door, opened it and called.

"Hello?"

No Answer. Angelos went inside. No one there. Next room. Nothing. Next ...

Angelos froze.

Safiye lay weeping on the ground. In a huge pool of blood.

A shot in the head.

Then Angelos got a hit on his head.

49

As Angelos awakened, his head roared. Parts of the visual field were missing.

Fact 1: I'm laying on the ground.

Fact 2: I am tied up.

Fact 3: Safiye lies in a pool of blood next to me.

Instinctively Angelos tried to open the cable ties.

"Do not waste your time, Nikakis!"

At first Angelos only saw the legs. But he knew the voice. It was Wolfe.

"Untie me", Angelos yelled.

"That might suit you. No. You will stay here until the Emiratis arrive. Then your problems will start. The princess was killed by you and your weapon was used and lies next to the body of the victim. It's pretty clear, right?", Wolfe said.

"You should never let strangers into your house. They could accidentally find a weapon and take it with them!"

Wolfe laughed.

"Who the hell are you in reality?", Angelos asked, still dazed by the beating.

"My name is Clarke. And I really work for the FBI. However, I still have a co-employer, so to speak! Or better: two. "

"Why? Why did you kill the girl? You wanted that the Emir to gives up the gas fields. You have achieved that. Or better AEXCOM, right? "

"Pretty close. They were not thrilled in Houston about your show. Then we thought how to kick Sharjah off the pitch and break your neck at the same time!"

"Why should I kill the princess?", Angelos asked.

"Because of the diamonds. Little cop and the temptation! "

"That's absolutely ridiculous. Nobody will believe you!"

"For real? And anyway: it does not matter! "

Angelos realized that his survival was not part of the plan.

Alex, you should come soon.

Then Angelos understood.

"For AEXCOM it was a success, as the Emir declared his change of policy. Then the release should have been done. But you work for a third party!"

Wolfe, or better Clarke, laughed.

"Finally. Yes, and what is the consequence of all this?

The world will learn about the murder of the princess in an hour - and that AEXCOM was the contractee. Once again they will be in middle of a hurricane and the Emir will seek revenge.

Both are out of the game. And the highest bidder has won "

"I suppose Moscow. And that's why everything came to the public. First ,kaloqueen' and then the leak about the handover. All your work!", Angelos said wearily.

"You never intended that the princess wIll survive, you fucking asshole!"

"You are right. She had no chance. Only with a dead princess both would be out of the game: Houston and Sharjah. Ah, the gentlemen are coming! "

The two Emiratis stormed into the room and looked horrified at the corpse.

"He murdered her, I have seen it," Wolfe/Clarke said.

Immediately, the two began to beat Angelos. Into the stomach, against the head. They would undoubtedly have killed him if Alex wouldn´t have arrived in that moment. He saw Angelos on the ground, drew his pistol and shot from the front door at the young Emirati. The bullet hits.

The man slammed against the wall, hit in the shoulder. But before Alex could shoot again, he heard a voice.

"Weapon on the ground, Alex. And slowly push it in the direction of the room. I aim for your husband's head! "

Wolfe, Alex thought.

He had no choice but to put the Glock on the floor and push it towards the room.

"Come in!"

Alex gasped as he entered the room. Safiye dead on the ground. And a groaning Angelos writhing in pain. Alex wanted to kneel.

"Go to the corner, Alex. That's good. Now we call the Crown Prince. He will be thrilled that the killer is caught!"

"You are a cowardly murderer. Have you had henchmen to do that?", Alex asked.

"I can rely on my Pashtuns. And they already disappeared!"

"Alex, please be quiet", Angelos said in pain.

Then Alex heard Khaled arriving and running to the house.

"Safiye!"

When he entered the room and saw his sister lying dead on the ground, he screamed like a bewildered animal and dropped to his knees.

The uninjured Emirati began to persuade the Crown Prince and pointed several times at Angelos.

Although Alex did not understand a word, it was clear that the Emirati was accusing Angelos.

"Your Highness, I was here", Wolfe alias Clarke said.

Khaled nodded.

Alex did not know how to address Khaled.

"This is ridiculous. He did everything to save the princess. He knew her. They liked each other. Why should he do that? Where is the motive?"

"The motive is in the bag", Wolfe said.

Completely petrified, Khaled said:

"Take him to my villa!"

The Emirati and Wolfe pulled Angelos up and dragged him to the car.

"He is Greek. You have no right ... ", Alex yelled, but he could not do anything. Wolfe had his pistol and kept him in check.

They will not let Angelos stay alive, he thought, and Alex was shaking.
After all, I know where to go.
After the car with Angelos drove off with screeching tires, Alex also ran to the car.
I do not have a weapon. What should I do?

50

Alex sped down to Kalafati. As he stopped in front of the "Villas", he just saw the Emirati and Wolfe drag Angelos to the mansion. There they threw him to the ground.
The Crown Prince stood by, seemingly untouched.
"Your Highness. At least listen to him!" Alex pleaded.
Khaled snapped at the Emirati and then the Emirati gave Khaled his weapon.
Khaled pointed it on Angelos. No, I will not watch him dying. Alex lost consciousness...
So, he could not see how the Crown Prince shot the Emirati and then Wolfe / Clarke in their heads.
Khaled leaned down to Angelos.
"Are you all right?"
"I've been better. The kicks were really bad. But thanks for helping me! "
Khaled freed Angelos from the bonds.

As they faced each other Khaled tried to kiss Angelos, but Angelos turned slightly aside.

"I'm sorry. I could not save your sister. She was a remarkable woman", Angelos said dejectedly.

"It was not your fault. But she was responsible that I met you. I will be grateful for the rest of my life. Without her …"

Only now Angelos saw that Alex was still laying unconscious on the ground.

"Arkoudaki! Wake up, I'm still alive", Angelos whispered in Alex' ear.

"You love him very much, right?", Khaled asked.

"Oh yeah!"

"But you keep your promise?", Khaled asked. Angelos hesitated.

"Yes. Even if I do not understand …,but I always keep my promises!"

Now two were smiling. Khaled and Alex, who gained back consciousness.

"I was so scared", Alex said softly.

"Me too", Angelos answered.

"What are we going to do with the bodies?", Angelos asked.

"I have a helicopter coming. He is on stand-by. To bring Safiye home, but now ... She must be buried before sunset. What do you think about, if the two other corpses would fall out of the helicopter in a turbulence?"

'That's a great idea", Angelos said.

"Well. See you at 9 pm?", Khaled asked.

Angelos just nodded.

51

"YOU DID WHAT? "Alex shouted across the beach.
"I called Khaled before the handover and told him that I do not trust Wolfe. He left shortly after you to drive to Merchias again. He wanted to see what's going on there. At least he would be able to tell me how many kidnappers are there and which car they drive, he said. He has promised not to intervene. I was quite right that he would not get in my way. Only: according to the tracking system he did not drive to Merchias. He always stayed south of the dam. So near Ano Mera. But when I saw it on the notebook, I could not react. Two minutes later, the call came with the instruction to throw the bag out of the car. And I could not wait for you!"
"... because I was still on the way", Alex added.
"I warned Khaled that I do not know what to do and that I don´t know if she is still alive. He said that he trusts me, and he will intervene if necessary: under one condition or request. If he would save my life - and only then -, uh, .."

"AND YOU SAID YES?"

"Fuck. I was hoping that I would be wrong and despite Wolfe everything goes well. Then I would not have needed Khaled. The second option was you. If you would have come in time ... but you could not. It was just the last, the third option. I was pretty desperate and would have promised him everything."

After a short break Angelos said:

"He saved my life. You were there. Wolfe would have killed me. I had no weapon and was tied up."

"No, no and no again", Alex said angrily.

"You would prefer that they would have killed me?", Angelos asked.

"Bullshit. But it is shabby to demand something like this!"

"Come on. You have committed a murder out of love. I love you and nothing will change that. He is in love with me and not the other way around!"

"I'm supposed to accept that you sleep with another man because of honor?"

"I have promised it. But more importantly, it's because of him, that we are still alive and you have someone to love!"

Alex grumbled.

"Do you think he loves you less after having sex with you?"

"No, but that does not interest me. Sex without love is not for me. It will not be what he expects!"
"You underestimate your abilities", Alex said.

Angelos laughed.
"Certain things I do only with you!"
And after a short break, he added:
"Do you think he would leave us alone otherwise?"
"He'll be even more in love afterwards", Alex replied.
"But not if I hurt him!"

52

"I love you, Angelos! ", Khalid said.
"I know. That does not make it easier for me! "
"Do not say you did not enjoy it. That would be a lie! "
Yes. That would be a lie. You look damned good. You have charisma. Well and by the way: you are still a prince!
Great combination, Angelos thought.
"But it does not change anything. I could fall in love with you, yes. How should it work? We

would be hunted, in the truest sense. Besides, I'm a simple policeman on a small island! "
"Well, as big as Sharjah", Khalid said, smiling. "And then you forget one thing: I love Alex and I'll never leave him!"
'That rather encourages me. I will do nothing, not bother you. But I will do what you told me to do: wait. Even if it takes a long time. And then I'll be there to ask you again! "
"Even if Alex and I should go separate ways, that can take ten years. Until then you've met dozens of other men and you have forgotten me."
"Look at me, Angelos. Look into my eyes. What do you see?"
"Something that scares me", Angelos answered.
"Is it your brain which tells you, you should stay with Alex or your heart? One must not mix up gratitude with love. He helped you a lot, but he got something for that! "
'The most beautiful mayor of Greece!", Angelos laughed.
"Sorry, that was for insiders", he added.
"You are self-confident, I like that!"
"I'm not what you think. I have sleepless nights, screaming. There is nothing left of the self-confident Angelos!"
"Why? A trauma?", Khaled asked.

Angelos hesitated. But Khaled radiated so much confidence and honest interest.

"I was raped by three men when I was 25!"
Khaled looked dumbfounded.
"Oh God. And I force you to have sex. It ... I'm
sorry."
After a break he said:
"Safiye has described the evening as the
most beautiful day of her life. And for me, this
night was the best of my life!"
Yes, Angelos thought, it was special. You
really devoured me. And in yours
One can read one's eyes: love. And
dedication. And most of all, hope.
"Khaled, I have to go home!"
"Didn´t the night made you think?"
"Yes, it did. Already the kiss three days ago
touched and confused me. But I could never
do that to Alex. He would break. I know that!"
"As I said, gratitude is not enough!"
Is it really just gratitude?
"Please stay another half hour. You would
make me very happy,", Khaled said softly.
And Angelos stayed longer.

When he got tired, he pulled himself up.
I have to go home.
Then he saw that he had received a text
message.
An hour ago. Alex.
"Where are you? Please do not leave me.
ILY"
"Oh shit", Angelos said, jumped out of bed
and hastily pulling on his pants.

"What is it?", Khaled asked.

Angelos just said: "Alex."

Outside, he tapped the answer in his cell phone.

"I will be home soon. Chill out. I'll never leave you. Your Emir."

A thousand thoughts flashed through his head as he drove.

Alex knew it. I ASKED him. And he agreed. Khaled had not only saved Angelo's life, but Alex' as well. And it would only be sex, Angelos said a few hours ago.

I should have left after the first time, Angelos thought. Do I stay just because of obligation or gratitude? And: am I in love with Khaled? I don't know. But it's true: I would not leave Alex.

When he arrived in Ornos after an endless journey, he ran into the house. The kitchen looked like a battlefield. Two notebooks and the Espresso machine on the ground. Crashed.

Angelos ran up the stairs and stormed into the bedroom.

"ALEX!"

But Alex did not answer.

Is he sleeping or ...?

Then he saw the ampoule. Insulin.

As a commissioner, you know how to kill yourself. Painless.

Angelos could have screamed. He could not.

Check the pulse. Call. Come on. But he was paralyzed.

I took a minute to take back control. Angelos still felt a weak pulse. Then he reached for the cell phone. Come on! "Andre? Please come immediately. Alex injected himself insulin!"

Only two minutes later André arrived with screeching tires. When he saw Alex lying there, he said to Angelos:

"You stupid, stupid asshole. I wish you would lay there! Dead! "

Next to be released:

At first, the gay Chief commissioner and Mayor Angelos Nikakis does not believe it: a golf course is to be built on the dry island of Mykonos. When Nikakis meets the investor, he thinks he knows him. Before he remembers, two murders happen.
Meanwhile, Angelos' husband Alex finds out why Angelos knows the investor.
Soon a third murder will happen. And the culprit is Alex.

Already published in GERMAN and GREEK:

Paul Katsitis – Der Putsch

1967 putscht in Griechenland das Militär.
Hellas und auch Mykonos ächzen unter der
Diktatur.
52 Jahre später gibt es wieder einen
Regierungswechsel in Athen. Doch die
Ereignisse von damals werfen ihre späten
Schatten.
Ein Flugzeugabsturz und Kommissar Angelos
Nikakis sorgen dafür, dass es zu einem
politischen Erdbeben kommt.

Paul Katsitis – Glut

Der Alptraum aller Chora-Bewohner wird
wahr. Ein Großbrand wütet in den engen
Gassen der Stadt. Eine knifflige Aufgabe
nicht nur für die Feuerwehr, sondern auch
für Kommissar und Bürgermeister Angelos
Nikakis. Denn in einem Haus findet man
eine Leiche. Ein Brandopfer, denken viele.
Doch sie wurde erschossen. Drei weitere
Morde und der Wiederaufbau lassen
Angelos kaum Zeit Luft zu holen.

Paul Katsitis - Abseits

Im Stadion von Mykonos wird die Leiche eines Mannes gefunden. Da der Mann Fan von Olympiakos Piräus war, geraten alle Anhänger des Konkurrenzvereins Panathinaikos Athen in Verdacht. Die Indizien lassen zunächst keine andere These zu und der Hass zwischen beiden Lagern ist tatsächlich so groß, dass auch ein Mord im Bereich des Möglichen liegt.
Doch als Kommissar Angelos Nikakis in die Welt der Spielerscouts eintaucht, stellt er fest, dass es um ganz andere Dinge ging: um Menschenhandel, Pädophilie und natürlich eine Menge Geld!

Paul Katsitis – Die Maske

ohne Vorwarnung in den Rücken geschossen hat, steht er bald unter Anklage.
Im Schatten des Prozesses gelingt es einem neuen, besonders brutalen Drogenhändler, genannt „Máská", sein Netzwerk auszubauen. Und er zögert auch nicht, als sich ihm die Gelegenheit bietet, Kommissar a.D. Angelos Nikakis aus dem Weg zu räumen.

Paul Katsitis – Die Bestie von Mykonos

Zwei Kriminalbeamte, Alexandros und Angelos, quittieren den Dienst und eröffnen gemeinsam auf Mykonos eine Bar. Nebenher betreiben sie eine kleine Privat-Detektei. Da die Polizei chronisch unterbesetzt ist, werden Alex und Angelos – wegen ihrer Erfahrung - regelmäßig hinzugezogen.
Mykonos ist in Aufruhr. Offensichtlich foltert, vergewaltigt und tötet ein Mann junge Touristen. Um ihn zu stellen, bleibt nichts anderes übrig, als dass Angelos den Lockvogel spielt – mit furchtbaren Konsequenzen ...

Paul Katsitis – Rache

Im Kloster Ano Mera auf Mykonos wird ein Priester tot aufgefunden, dessen Leiche übel zugerichtet ist. Es sieht nach einem Rachemord aus – doch wofür?

Paul Katsitis - Hass

Es ist ein besonderer Fall für die beiden Ermittler Alex und Angelos Nikakis. Die Leiche eines jungen Mannes wird in den Dünen gefunden. Am und im Körper des Toten findet sich die DNA von Angelos.

Er wird verhaftet. Zuerst geschockt von der Möglichkeit, dass Angelos Es ist ein besonderer Fall für die beiden ihn betrogen hat, beschließt Alex, den Beweisen nicht zu glauben.
Und hat Recht. Hinter allem steht nur eines:

Paul Katsitis – Inzest

Ein Bräutigam, der sich am Tag der Hochzeit vom Balkon stürzt und eine Mädchenleiche in einer Wagenpresse. Zwei Fälle für die beiden Ex-Kommissare Alex und Angelos Nikakis Zwei Fälle, die sich nach und nach aufeinander zu bewegen.

Paul Katsitis – Der-Drei-Sterne-Mord

Im besten Restaurant der Insel wird der Chefkoch, ehemals Leibkoch Gaddafis, mit durchschnittener Kehle aufgefunden. Ein schwieriger Fall für Alex und Angelos, zumal die eigene Familie mit beteiligt ist. Der Fall erfährt eine erstaunliche Wendung, als die beiden Ermittler erfahren, dass der britische Außenminister Mykonos besucht – auf dem Landsitz des griechischen Premierministers.

Paul Katsitis - Tattoo

Zwei Highlights stehen auf dem Programm des Wochenendes: ein hochdotiertes Beachvolleyball-Turnier und die Eröffnung der ersten Spielbank auf der Insel.
Nicht ins „Event-Wochenende" passen zwei Tote: ein 19-jähriger Junge und einer der Beachvolleyballspieler. An dessen „natürlichem Tod" haben die Ermittler Alex und Angelos so ihre Zweifel.

Paul Katsitis – Skalpell
Am Strand von Ornos wird eine Frauenleiche gefunden. Es ist die Tochter des Bürgermeisters. Der Leiche fehlen Nieren und Leber.
Doch es geht bei der Mordserie nicht nur um Organe, wie die beiden Ermittler Alexandros und Angelos Nikakis bald feststellen. Es existiert ein komplexes Netzwerk, das verschiedene kriminelle Felder abdeckt, und so mancher Inselbewohner ist darin verstrickt.